# Bestias

S.A.O

Tranquility Hub Limited

Bestias

# PROLOGUE

I used to love science fiction, but as a genre of a movie or book, not my life. Six years ago, that all changed. I still love science fiction but in a different way, a more primal way.

# CHAPTER ONE

## HOW IT STARTED FOR ME

**Taranis**

For months, the news had been filled with reports of rampaging animals killing people, but these weren't ordinary animals. They were changed—modified into grotesque, unnatural forms. Despite the disturbing stories, Dad dismissed it all as conspiracy theories.

"Don't worry," he said, brushing it off. "It's just a city thing, son." He avoided my gaze as he said it, his usual way of hiding his worries. I wanted to remind him that I'd soon be heading to university in that very city, but the words caught in my throat.

The strange events began with an earthquake. Earthquakes were common in our small town, but this one was different. By the next morning, all the farm animals had vanished without a trace.

Bruno, our usually calm and gentle dog, was tense that night. His ears were pricked, and he growled at every sound. It felt like nowhere in or around the house was safe. My heart raced as I watched him pace, his nails scraping

1

the wooden floor.

Something was wrong—terribly wrong.

My parents chalked it up to the upcoming earthquake, saying the tell-tale signs were already showing. But nothing could calm Bruno, and his unease only fuelled my growing dread.

That night, I couldn't sleep. Beyond the walls of our house, I heard muffled thumps, low growls, and a single far-off scream. Bruno's pacing continued, restless and anxious. Whatever was out there, it was close.

The next morning, I was getting ready to go clean Mrs. Greene's house—a job I'd taken on every summer for the past five years. As I packed my things, several screams pierced the air outside, followed by Bruno's frantic barking. Ignoring his half-eaten food, he charged to the door. Dad grabbed his pistol and headed outside to check on the commotion. The sudden action made my heart race.

In our town, silence was the norm. Even during a robbery, people stayed quiet. The screams and chaos outside were unlike anything I'd ever heard. My mind whirled with fear as I struggled to make sense of it all. "It takes a second for your whole reality to come crashing down." I used to think understanding that phrase would somehow protect me from its truth. But nothing could have prepared me for what happened next. The air filled with a sharp, sulfuric smell as I watched in horror—my mother's skin melted off her face, down to the bone. Her scream, once human, morphed into something monstrous.

"Mother?!" I choked out, my voice a hoarse whisper of disbelief. Another scream erupted from inside the house, followed by Bruno's frantic barking.

Dad hadn't even made it to the door. He turned back, grabbing my arm and yanking me away from the gruesome scene. The new scream—the one that ripped through my own throat—was something I didn't even recognize at first. Tears blurred my vision as my face burned with the intensity of fear and grief.

Dad shoved my backpack into my arms and barked an order at Bruno to follow me. Obedient as always, Bruno pulled me away from the house. I caught a glimpse of the pistol in Dad's hand as he slammed the door shut, flashing me a loving smile for just a second before disappearing back inside. My mother's screams, now nothing more than inhuman gurgles, echoed in the air.

I could only describe it as a worm the size of a German shepherd. Its body was covered in dark, pulsing spots that oozed some kind of acidic liquid. It had no discernible mouth, just a grotesque mass of flesh and venom. I stood frozen in place for what felt like an eternity, trying to process what I'd just witnessed. But there was no time to react—no time to try to help. Bruno tugged at my pants, urging me to move, but all I could do was stare at the house that had once been my home.

Why? Why was Bruno pulling me away? My mother was in there, in pain, and my father… what about my father? I yanked my pants free from his grip, anger bubbling up from deep inside me. How could my loyal companion abandon them like this? How could I?

I nearly turned back toward the house, my hand reaching for the doorknob. But then, a gunshot rang out from just behind the door, jolting me back to reality. What am I doing? I can't do anything in there. I couldn't even help when it all happened right in front of me. I just stood there, crying like a useless bystander.

A sharp twinge of pain shot through my leg, pulling me out of my thoughts. I looked down and saw that Bruno had bitten me—a little too close to my leg. His teeth had scraped the skin, drawing a bit of blood. I let Bruno pull me away from the house, my body moving automatically as my mind swirled with confusion and guilt.

He tugged at my trousers a few more times, checking to see if I would resist again, but I didn't. I followed him as we moved further away from the house and into the town.

A shiver ran down my spine as I realized my house wasn't the only one that had been attacked. The destruction spread far and wide, and yet, I hadn't seen anyone else.

The eerie emptiness of the town weighed heavily on me as I carefully stepped around splinters of wood and shards of glass, hoping to avoid making any noise. Not that the worm could hear me—at least, I note. The town school came into view, triggering memories of being left out and ignored by my classmates. For a brief moment, I almost felt a sense of satisfaction at the thought that some of them might be gone. But that feeling was quickly overshadowed by the grim reality of it all. I didn't miss anyone except for Mrs. Greene and my parents.

The overwhelming urge to turn back gnawed at me. My father shouldn't have to fight alone. Why was I walking away from him? I should have protested, should have tried to help. But instead, my feet carried me farther and farther away, until I broke into a run when a loud crash came from the house beside me. Bruno barked wildly beside me, urging me forward.

"I'm scum. I'm scum. I'm scum." The words pounded in my head with each step. I ran until my lungs burned and my legs turned to jelly.

Eventually, my strength gave out, and I stumbled to a stop in front of a half-collapsed house. Bruno barked again, pulling me away from it and in the opposite direction. My body complied, though my mind was still reeling with thoughts of escape—escape from that horrific thing I should have helped to subdue, escape from the reality of my pathetic life.

Looking round I realised I had stopped in front of Ms. Greene's house, unable to take another step. I decided to go in remembering then that I had a spare key since I took care of the house and determined it was safe since Bruno followed me quietly.

Luckily the interior was not badly damaged, I guess the monster—that's what that thing looked like, not like any animal I'd ever seen just a monster—had skipped this house since it was empty—a few things were toppled over like the flower vase I got her three years ago and a few papers and books—, Ms. Greene was with her family in the city—and she wouldn't mind me staying here during such a crisis.

I looked around carefully and sighed with relief when I found no signs of a break-in or animal trails—it was the earthquake that had toppled over those things, the usual homey smell however was compromised by the smell of dust and dried cement.

I walked towards the garden—past the living room and through the sliding door—-determined to grab a weapon, Ms. Greene's husband, like almost all other men in town, was a hunter.

It was a hobby and pastime here, most times they used non-lethal methods just so they could release them once caught.

I moved as quickly and silently as I could towards the shed—-the musty smell was welcomed as it calmed and irritated me at the same time—-opening it I looked around for the handle in the wall that opened the door to his arsenal and collection of weapons, and then picked a shotgun, 'that'll do', but then I thought against that as it would be too loud, an axe might be the way, but I don't want to have to get close to anything like that worm, let's just take a rifle with a suppressor, I grabbed the one that Mr. Greene had used to 'teach' me once—I hadn't touched a firearm since then.

My hands trembled as I held the weapon in my hands, weighing it and wondering if this was the best course of action.

In an impromptu moment of foolish bravery, or plain foolishness, I decided to try and go back. To say goodbye to my mom, and at east know what had become of my heroic father.

...

It didn't take long before I was opening the door to my house, my nerves now back on edge, my once calm heartbeat rising once again---I thought of leaving Bruno at Mrs. Greene's but he had refused to stay, so I brought him along. So far, he had been dead quiet. I took it as his way of showing he understood what was happening and just how much it mattered to not expose ourselves by carelessly making noise—half expecting acid to spray me in the face as I opened the door. However, I was met with silence, which scared me even more. The door opened easily, and I slipped in first, Bruno not far behind, I took in the carnage before me—furniture overturned, the remnants of a once homely space now upturned. The smell and feel of home were gone, replaced by the pungent odour of sulphur.

As I moved further into the living room, a sound beneath my foot made my heart lurch. A sickening crack— like joints popping—echoed in the silence. I froze, dread tightening my chest as I slowly lowered my gaze.

There, amidst the chaos was a grim sight. My mother, or what remained of her, laid inert on the floor. The lower half of her body was a skeletal frame, with pieces of cloth clinging to brittle bones.

The upper half was nowhere to be seen.

"Bruno," I whispered, my voice barely a rasp. The dog pressed closer, his warm presence a little comfort against the harsh reality before me. Grief washed over me, threatening to drown my senses. Memories of her laughter, her gentle touches flooded my mind—I remembered the last time my mom laughed, her eyes sparkling as she helped me with homework. It felt like a lifetime ago—before being swallowed by her last moments and the image before me.

...

"Bruno," I repeated, this time more firmly, trying to ground myself in the present, seeking solace in his unwavering loyalty. His presence was the only thing tethering me to reality in the middle of the nightmare that had become my life.

With a heavy heart, I forced myself to rise. I couldn't stay here, surrounded by the remnants of a life that was now shattered beyond repair. I couldn't let my grief paralyze me. I had to move forward. I had to find my father.

I searched the house, each step heavy with dread, but I found no sign of him. There were bullet holes in the walls, overturned furniture, and signs of a struggle. He had fought back—of course he had—but where was he now? Was he dead, alive, or something in between? My mind raced with possibilities, but I couldn't let myself dwell on them. Not yet.

With trembling hands, I buried what remained of my mother in the backyard.

I didn't let myself think too much about what I was doing; I just focused on the task at hand, aggressively wiping away tears as I worked. Once it was done, I gathered supplies from the house—flashlights, a map, food, and a few clothes—and stuffed them into my backpack with shaky determination.

"I'll find him," I whispered to myself, my voice barely audible over the deafening silence that now enveloped our once serene home. Bruno stayed by my side, his silent presence offering me a small measure of comfort. He was the only thing keeping me from falling apart completely.

I had no idea where that thing had gone, but there was a crack in the ground leading up to the hole it had crawled out of. There were no signs of my father, and his gun wasn't anywhere to be found either. That gave me a flicker of hope—hope that he was still out there, somewhere, fighting.

It felt wrong—unnatural—that I hadn't seen anyone else outside. We were a small town, not many of us lived here, but the eerie emptiness was unnerving. I walked quietly back to Mrs. Greene's house, every step filled with the fear that the worm or something worse might still be out there, lurking in the shadows, waiting to strike.

Once inside, I barricaded all the entrances, pushing the sofa in front of the glass door that led to the garden and stacking chairs against the front door. The rest of the furniture joined the barricade after I sat down to plan my next move. I knew staying here wasn't a long-term solution. I'd have to leave eventually—get out of town and head as far away from the cities as possible. After all, that's where all of this had started.

I checked around the house one last time, making sure there were no threats, and then barricaded the stairs as well. I decided to stay downstairs, where it felt safer. I had enough bullets and rations to last me for a little while, but I knew I couldn't stay here forever. I made a plan to leave at dawn the next day, hoping to get some sleep in the meantime. But sleep was elusive, and I found myself lying awake, listening to every creak and groan of the house, every distant sound from outside. Eventually, exhaustion overtook me, and I fell into a restless sleep.

...

I jolted awake at some point, panic immediately setting in as I scanned my surroundings. Where was I? My mind raced, trying to piece together the fragments of memory from the day before. I called out for my mother, quietly at first, then louder. But the words died in my throat as the memories came flooding back, hitting me like a freight train.

She was gone. And I had no idea where my father was, or if he was even still alive. Sobs welled up in my chest, and I let them out, crying and wailing as the weight of it all came crashing down on me. My first source of protection was gone, and my second was lost to the chaos. Why? Why had this happened? Why didn't anyone listen when I said something felt off? And now, everyone was gone. The town was empty, and I was left alone in the aftermath.

Bruno's soft whimpers brought me back to reality. He nudged my hand, then slowly climbed onto me, attempting to lick away my tears in his own way of comforting me. I raised a trembling hand to his snout, then over his head, running my fingers through his soft fur before wrapping my arms around him and holding him close.

Bruno wasn't my mom, but in that moment, he was the only thread of hope and protection I had left.

"Thanks, Bruno," I whispered, my voice hoarse and broken. "Good boy."

As I held him, the weight of what lay ahead pressed down on me. I had no idea what was coming next, but I knew one thing: I couldn't stay here. I couldn't let whatever took my mother and destroyed my town take me too. I had to survive, for my father, for Bruno, and for myself.

And with that thought, I slowly began to plan for what's to come.

## CHAPTER TWO

## PEOPLE

My whole body ached, and my eyes stung. Bruno pressed his warm body against mine, a small comfort as sobs wracked my frame. Sleep had abandoned me, leaving me alone with my grief and the cold predawn air. When the sobs finally subsided, I whispered my thanks to him again, though I wasn't sure how much comfort words could bring either of us now. When morning came, I gave Bruno some of the dog food Ms. Greene kept at her house for him—something to fill his belly before we left. I didn't know where we were going, only that it needed to be away from the ruins of what my life had once been. Somewhere my father might have found refuge. Somewhere safer than this.

We walked for hours, the silence around us heavy with uncertainty. Bruno stayed close, his presence grounding me as my thoughts swirled with fear and hope in equal measure. We hadn't encountered anyone—no sign of life but the horrors that had consumed my town. But just as the quiet began to feel suffocating, Bruno started barking.

I jumped at the sudden noise, panic bubbling up

inside me. I shushed him quickly, fear taking hold. What if something dangerous heard us? What if —

I looked up, and dread flooded my chest. A Humvee was approaching, about 500 meters away. Instinctively, I grabbed Bruno's collar and tugged him toward me, trying to pull him away from the road.

"No, no, no," I muttered under my breath, my heart racing. Bruno resisted at first, barking at the vehicle, but I didn't let go. After a few tugs, he relented, and we broke into a run. Still, he kept turning back, barking intermittently— protecting me in the only way he knew how. It filled me with a bittersweet pride. He was trying so hard, but it also scared me. What if the people in that vehicle weren't friendly?

"Shit," I whispered as the Humvee sped up. My mind raced with scenarios—every book and movie I'd ever seen about the collapse of society flashed through my head. If there's one thing they all taught me, it's that people can be just as dangerous as monsters, if not more so.

"Stop!" someone shouted behind us, their voice echoing through the still air. But instead of stopping, I ran faster, desperation fuelling my steps. I knew I couldn't outrun the vehicle, but fear kept me going. Bruno stayed by my side, his pace matching mine as we fled.

The Humvee caught up to us in no time, skidding to a stop right in front of me. Frantically, I turned to run in the other direction, but I was stopped by a soldier who appeared out of nowhere. He held a gun up and pointed it at me. I froze, taking a step back, my heart pounding in my chest.

"Why did you run?" the soldier demanded, his voice a mix of suspicion and weary frustration. My throat closed up, and I couldn't find the words to answer him. My silence wasn't just born of fear—it was a small, defiant stand against the chaos that had swallowed my life. What did it matter why I ran? What could I even say that would make sense in this madness?

"What are you doing out here?" he pressed, his tone growing harsher. Still, I said nothing.

The slap came fast. A sharp sting exploded across my cheek, shocking me into silence even more. Bruno's growl built into a frenzied bark, his fierce loyalty unwavering. I wanted to stop him, to protect him from whatever would come next, but the words wouldn't come out.

A gunshot rang out.

Bruno's barking cut off, leaving a deafening silence in its wake. I turned, the world slowing down around me as I saw his limp body on the ground. Numbness washed over me, freezing me in place. A single sob tore from my throat, breaking the silence.

"No… no… not this…"

Despair overwhelmed me, pulling me down into a helpless heap on the cold, unyielding ground. I crawled to Bruno's side, my fingers trembling as I reached for him. My vision blurred as I tried to cry, but there were no tears left. I had already cried too much last night. Instead, I screamed—a raw, guttural release of all my pain and fear. I screamed as I squeezed Bruno's limp body, as I called out his name over and over again, each shout tearing my throat apart.

The taste of iron filled my mouth, but I didn't care.

Rough hands clamped around my wrists, wrenching me backward. Another set of hands tore Bruno from my weakening grip, dragging me away from him. I stumbled, half-resisting, half-pleading for them to let me go. But they didn't stop. They dragged me toward the looming shadow of the Humvee, and with each step, I felt another piece of myself break.

"Shut him up," the tallest one barked. Something heavy crashed into my skull, and the world went dark.

17

I jolted awake as icy water splashed over my face, sending a shock through my entire body. My eyes shot open, but the pain in my head made me squeeze them shut again. Slowly, I reopened them, trying to blink away the haze.

Two soldiers stood in front of me. The woman, who held the bucket, watched me with a bored expression, while her partner stood by with a gun in hand. My hands were bound tightly behind me, and my legs were strapped to either side of the cold metal chair I was sitting in.

"Are you awake?" the woman asked, though her voice lacked any real curiosity. It was flat, detached, as though my consciousness was just a minor inconvenience in her day, she dropped the bucket, it clanked against the ground and the sound echoed, the vibrations resonating through the floor.

I looked around, taking in my surroundings as best as I could. The small metal room was harsh and unwelcoming. The walls reflected the glare of a single fluorescent light that hung above me, and the sharp smell of disinfectant stung my nose, making my eyes water.

There were no windows, just a small rectangular

opening at the top of the door with metal bars across it. I couldn't see anything else, as the second soldier blocked most of my view. "Name," the woman grunted. I didn't respond. My head throbbed too much, and the bright light only made it worse. All I wanted was to be left alone, to not feel this pain anymore. "SPEAK!" she shouted, her voice echoing off the metal walls. "Lift your head. Answer me. What's wrong with him?"

I tried to lift my head, but it felt too heavy. The pounding in my skull was relentless, and I couldn't find the strength to fight against it. After a moment, I let my head drop again, a silent plea for them to just leave me alone.

The woman's patience wore thin. "DID YOU CUT OUT HIS TONGUE?!" she yelled, stepping forward and raising her hand as if to strike me again.

Instinctively, I squeezed my eyes shut, bracing for the impact.

"Enough," a voice interrupted, cutting through the tension. It was a man's voice, calm but firm. I couldn't see him from where I sat, but his presence was palpable. He stepped forward, his movements decisive. His hand had intercepted the woman's mid-air, lowering it with a firm grip. "Let's go. We'll come back when he's more lucid."

I caught a fleeting glimpse of his face as he glanced at me—a brief, intense look that I couldn't quite decipher — before he signalled the others to exit the room.

They left without another word, the door slamming shut behind them with a loud bang. The sound made me flinch, and I was left alone in the suffocating silence, still tied to the chair.

...

In the solitude of the cold metal room, I was left alone with my thoughts. I had lost everything in the blink of an eye. My mother had been reduced to a puddle before my eyes. My father was nowhere to be found. And my best friend— my loyal companion—had been shot down trying to protect me.

I couldn't even cry anymore. The pain had consumed me, numbed me to the point where all I could do was breathe. Each breath felt like a struggle against the overwhelming weight of grief that pressed down on me from all sides.

The room felt like a cage, every breath stinging with the sharp scent of disinfectant. I shifted in the chair, trying to alleviate the discomfort of the rough bindings around my wrists, but the cold metal only reminded me of my captivity. There was no escape from this—no escape from the horrors that had taken everything from me.

I clenched my fists as tightly as I could, frustration and fear battling for dominance in my mind. Why was this happening? Why had everything been ripped away from me in an instant? I tried to make sense of it, but nothing seemed real anymore. Everything was a blur of loss and pain.

They hadn't killed me yet, so that meant they wanted something from me. But what? Did they think I knew something about the monsters that had destroyed my town? Did they think I was part of whatever chaos had unfolded?

Various scenarios played out in my mind—being forced to join them, working until I collapsed from exhaustion, or worse.

The thoughts made me shiver, my muscles tensing with fear. I tried to stay awake, but exhaustion pulled at me, heavy and relentless. I had no idea what they wanted from me, or what awaited me once the soldiers returned. The fear of the unknown gnawed at my insides, threatening to consume me. Eventually, despite the cold, despite the pain, sleep claimed me.

...

When I woke again, I wasn't sure how much time had passed. The room was as cold and metallic as ever, but the dim light filtering through the small barred window on the door suggested that some time had slipped by. My wrists ached from the rough bindings, and my muscles protested any attempt at movement.

I listened carefully for any sounds outside the door. Footsteps echoed in the distance—sometimes faint, sometimes close—but I couldn't make out any specific words or voices. It was as if the world outside this tiny room was just as cold and distant as the one inside it.

For a long time, I sat in silence, my thoughts drifting between memories of what I had lost and the fear of what might come next. I wondered if I would ever get out of this place—if I would ever see my father again, or if the world had already swallowed him whole, just like it had everything else.

The door creaked open, and I flinched instinctively. Two soldiers entered, their expressions as unreadable as before. The man who had stopped the woman from hitting me earlier stood in the doorway, his gaze fixed on me with that same intensity.

"Time to talk," he said, his voice calm but with an undertone of authority. He motioned for the others to release my bindings. "We need answers."

I felt the tension in my body ease slightly as the rough ropes around my wrists and ankles were loosened, allowing blood to circulate freely once more. But the relief was short-lived, replaced by the creeping dread of what this "talk" would entail.

I didn't move from the chair as the man stepped closer. He knelt down, meeting my eyes at my level, his expression neutral but not unkind.

"What's your name?" he asked, his voice softer now, though it still held that undercurrent of control.

I hesitated, unsure whether to trust him. But what choice did I have? I was trapped, with no escape in sight.

"Taranis," I whispered, my voice hoarse from disuse.

"Taranis," he repeated, as if testing the name on his tongue.

"Good. Now, Taranis, I need you to tell me what happened in your town."

My chest tightened at the mention of my home. Images of my mother, of Bruno, flashed through my mind, bringing fresh waves of grief crashing down on me. I

23

swallowed hard, fighting to keep my composure. "They weren't animals. They were... something else." "There were... monsters," I managed to choke out.

"They killed everyone."

The man nodded, as if he had expected this answer. "And your father? Do you know where he is?"

This question shook me, how did he know about my father? Did they search my house, how?

I shook my head, the motion making my head throb again. "I don't know. I don't know if he's alive."

Silence hung in the air between us for a moment before the man stood up, motioning to the other soldiers. "Keep him here for now," he said to them. "He's not a threat."

As they turned to leave, I called out to him, desperation creeping into my voice. "What... what happens now?"

The man paused at the doorway, glancing back at me with an expression I couldn't read. "You'll find out soon enough, Taranis. For now, rest. We'll talk more later."

And with that, the door shut once more, leaving me alone in the cold, metallic room.

Rest, he had said. But how could I rest when

everything I knew had been ripped away from me? How could I rest when the world had turned into a nightmare, and I was trapped in the middle of it?

I slowly slid onto the floor and curled up, letting my mind wander.

But despite my racing thoughts, exhaustion soon claimed me once again. I slipped into a restless sleep, my dreams filled with the faces of those I had lost, and the horrors I had witnessed.

I didn't know what tomorrow would bring. I didn't know if I would ever find my father, or if the world outside had any hope left. But for now, all I could do was survive. And that was all that mattered.

## CHAPTER THREE

## IN CAPTIVITY

I stayed silent for the next few days, only raising my head to see who came in but never speaking a word.

After the nicer soldier had left the others had come back to restrain me to the chair once more.

They threatened me for answers, answers I had already given—some with insults, others with more direct methods. The worst days were when the woman came. She used me as her punching bag, her fists landing blow after blow until my body was sore and bruised.

Somehow, the other soldiers found out about it because occasionally, they would come alone at night, taking turns relieving their stress on me. My existence had been reduced to enduring their cruelty.

I knew the days were passing because the lights went out every night, leaving me in darkness. Occasionally, someone would bring me food and stand watch while I relieved myself in a bucket they provided. It was humiliating, degrading, but I had no fight left in me. I didn't know how long it had been—a week, maybe?—but my body felt numb, a dull ache that never seemed to fade. I was tired—so tired—and I wanted it to end. Some part of me hoped they would let me go, but deep down, I knew better.

Today, a soldier entered alone, carrying a chair. It was the same one who had intervened before—the voice I had come to recognize. He often lingered in the background while the others interrogated me, but he was conspicuously absent when the woman took over. He was the only one who seemed to care enough to stop them from harming me, even if it was only one occasion.

"You woke up on your own today," he said, his voice neutral.

I didn't respond, just kept staring at the floor, too drained to care. Silence hung between us for a long moment before he sighed and made to stand up.

"You—they killed him… they killed him," I managed to croak out, my throat raw from days of screaming and from the meagre amounts of water they had given me. My voice was barely above a whisper, but it was enough to stop him in his tracks.

His face was hidden behind the same mask and goggles as the others, so I couldn't see if he was shocked. He just stared at me for a moment before speaking again.

"Good to know you can still talk," he said, more to himself than to me. "You mean your dog?"

I nodded slowly, the movement making my sore muscles protest. I had been tied up for what felt like an eternity, and my body had grown weak from it.

"I was told it was a nuisance," he said, the words cold and detached, as if that somehow justified what they had done. I winced slightly at his choice of words. "He," I corrected, though my voice lacked any real force. Bruno wasn't some nuisance—he was my friend, my protector. But to them, he was just an inconvenience, something to be discarded without a second thought.

The soldier didn't say anything for a long time. Then, finally, he spoke, his voice softer. "I'm sorry. I can't do any more for you."

I nodded again, a slow, mechanical movement. What more could I say? He stood up and left without another word, the door clicking shut behind him. I watched him leave, retreating into my own thoughts. He didn't even let me finish.

...

When I woke up again, it was the woman in front of me this time. Her mask was off, and she sat on the chair the other soldier had left behind.

"What's your name?" she asked, her voice oddly calm compared to the last time we had spoken, was this the same madwoman who only cared about releasing her frustration on me?

I didn't reply. I didn't trust her. She had hit me so many times before—why should I talk to her now? But she wasn't angry this time. She didn't lash out at me. Instead, she just looked at me, waiting.

"You are Taranis, right?" she asked, as if she didn't already know the answer. When I remained silent, she sighed and stood up. "Well, I'll be back tomorrow," she said, leaving the room.

She came back the next day, and the day after that. Each time, she hit me less. It was unsettling. I didn't know what had changed, but I couldn't bring myself to trust her newfound calmness. Still, eventually, I found myself speaking, telling her that I lived in a town not far from where they had taken me.

"Where's the other soldier?" I asked her as she was leaving one day.

She paused, her hand on the door handle. "That is not your concern," she said sharply, and with that, she was gone.

...

The next time I woke up, I was in a different place. It was a larger room, still made of cold metal, but this one had a huge glass window opposite me—a one-way window, I guessed. My hands were bound by my sides, and my legs were strapped to the metal chair I now sat in.

I heard a click as the door opened, and a woman in a lab coat walked in, followed by a man dressed the same. Both of them carried clipboards, ready to take notes.

"Begin," a voice said over what I assumed was an intercom. The woman stepped forward, producing a syringe filled with a colourless liquid. She crossed the room quickly and carefully pierced my skin with the needle, injecting the liquid into my arm.

A few minutes ticked by, but nothing happened. The woman sighed and turned to leave. The man simply stared at me, scribbling something on his clipboard before following her out.

I caught a glimpse of her nametag as she walked out.

"Tracy."

A short while later, she returned, this time with another syringe filled with the same clear liquid. She repeated the process, but this time, the reaction was immediate. Searing hot pain shot through my body, and I managed only a slight whimper before the world went black.

Following that episode, they relocated me to a larger room. For the next two days, they took me back to the lab and administered the clear liquid again, but to their confusion, it had no effect. The doctors seemed perplexed, but for me, it was a small victory—a brief moment of relief in an otherwise endless cycle of pain.

...

Today, however, they injected me with a light green liquid before the usual clear one. The moment it entered my veins, a sudden chill swept over me, followed by another wave of excruciating pain. This time, I cried out, unable to hold it in. My body jerked and spasmed uncontrollably, and I could feel and smell the blood as it leaked from my ears, eyes, and nose. My vision blurred, clouded by the red colour of my own blood. I shut my eyes tight, trying to ride out the pain, but it only grew worse.

31

The pain didn't stop. It just kept building and building until I thought I might go insane. My body eventually stopped spasming, but I still twitched every few minutes.

My breathing slowed, each inhale shaky and shallow, and my hearing grew worse. Everything became a muffled, warped cacophony, the sounds around me blending into an unintelligible mess.

I stayed like that for what felt like an eternity, unmoving, until my brain finally shut down, and I blacked out.

'Not again. No more,' I wanted to scream, but the words only echoed in my mind. I felt like I had lost the ability to speak, though my shrieks of pain during each test reminded me that I still had my voice—if only to express the agony they forced upon me.

The days blurred together after that. I surrendered to them, to the endless cycle of tests and pain. They had free reign over me now. I was their puppet, their plaything.

"I'm sorry, Mother, Father," I thought, my mind drifting in and out of consciousness. "I couldn't protect you."

And with that, I let the darkness take me once more.

## CHAPTER FOUR

## LIFE AS IT IS

For the first time in what felt like forever, I woke up in the stark confines of my assigned room. My body refused to cooperate—I couldn't sit up or even shift my position. The draining ordeal I had endured left me both physically weakened and emotionally numb. I scanned my sterile surroundings, and unsurprisingly, nothing had changed. It was the same cold, lifeless space. Oddly, I wasn't hungry, though I couldn't remember the last time I'd eaten.

As I lay there, memories surged like an unstoppable tide. Every time I closed my eyes, my mother's contorted face haunted me—her final moments forever etched into my mind. Bruno's lifeless body, too, weighed on me. His once-bright eyes, now vacant and gone. The pain was visceral. Every memory was like a knife twisting in my chest, leaving me breathless and hollow.

All I yearned for now was to find my father. Why had all this happened?

...

When I woke again, I managed to stir, albeit slightly. My body ached, but I forced myself to move. In a rare moment of curiosity, I reached into my pockets. My fingers brushed over something small and metal. I pulled out—a dog tag inscribed with "Bruno."

The nice soldier had given it to me before leaving for a mission, wishing me luck before he disappeared. I never learned his name. Now I hoped he would come back, though the world outside seemed no safer than the prison I was in.

A solitary tear traced a path down my cheek, surprising me. I thought I had no more tears left to cry. After countless nights of sobbing myself to sleep or succumbing to the mercy of pain-induced unconsciousness, I thought I was empty. But I wasn't.

Not yet.

. . .

The injections--I was tired of them. After about six more tests with the green liquid, they began injecting me with a deep red liquid. Its colour was too dark to be human blood, but I wasn't sure of anything anymore. Despite the new liquids, the clear one remained the most frequent—

administered every day like clockwork.

The light green liquid didn't cause the violent spasms it once did.

My body had learned to endure it. But the new brown liquid that followed...it was a different kind of hell. Each time it entered my bloodstream, it felt like molten lava. My insides burned, every nerve igniting with searing pain.

I writhed in agony, unable to escape the fire that spread through me.

But the red liquid... that was the worst of all. It wasn't as frequent, but each time it was administered, I gave up trying to hold back my screams. I would struggle, beg them not to inject me, but it never worked.

Today, though, the injection was only the clear liquid. An unexpected reprieve from the agony of the other substances. I savoured the brief moment of calm, my body craving any semblance of normalcy. But I knew better than to believe it would last. Moments of peace in this hell were fleeting, always followed by something worse.

"Tomorrow, we commence physical testing to ascertain Subject 3's utility in combat scenarios," Dr. Simmons' voice echoed through the intercom. His tone was clinical and detached, like he was talking about a piece of equipment rather than a human being.

Lydia escorted me back to my room, her presence cold and professional. I looked around the hallway, noticing for the first time that, despite the rows of similar iron doors on this floor, it was eerily silent. I might be the only subject here. A sudden, resonant thud vibrated through the floor as I crossed the threshold into my room, sending a shiver up my spine. My nerves, already frayed, went on high alert. Lydia shoved me inside, slamming the door behind me. I climbed into bed, ignoring the food they had left on the floor as usual, and fell into a fitful sleep.

…

The next day, as promised, the physical tests began. Dawn broke, casting a grey light into the spare room. My chest tightened as the realization hit me: today, they would push me beyond anything I'd experienced before.

Persistent knocks woke me. Groggy, I dragged myself toward the door.

"You're awake. Good," came a familiar voice through the bars. I recognized the voice; it was the nice soldier from before. He wasn't wearing a mask or helmet like the others. His black, wavy hair fell to his shoulders. I avoided making eye contact.

"I'll open the door so you can go wash up, okay?" he said, his voice gentle, almost apologetic.

"Okay," I whispered.

When the door unlatched, he stood there, studying me. His gaze lingered on me for a moment, but I ignored it, clutching my blue jumpsuit tightly to my chest, my eyes falling to his tag, 'Michael'. After a tense beat, he stepped aside, allowing me to pass. I didn't waste the opportunity, hurrying past him toward the bathroom.

Once dressed, Michael was waiting outside, looking somewhat anxious. He told me he was nervous but also excited about being assigned to me. This puzzled me, why was he nervous, what could possibly make him uncertain about being 'assigned' to me?

We made our way down the stairs, my thoughts swirling with memories of my lost family and the relentless injections. A new dread began to settle over me. The familiar sterile hallways gave way to the unknown depths of the base. Every step echoed, the silence amplifying my growing fear. This was no ordinary test.

We arrived at a large black-painted metal door. It led into a huge room that looked more like an arena than anything else. On the other side, a massive door loomed—far too large to be just an entrance for staff. A rhythmic thump of something came from the other side.

The arena's walls were made of a dark, absorbing material that seemed to swallow the light. The air was thick with the scent of metal and animal musk, making my stomach churn. Harsh fluorescent lights bathed the room in an unforgiving glow, casting long, eerie shadows across the floor. The man in the lab coat had mentioned physical tests, but an arena?

Michael must have sensed my fear. His voice was soft, a rare kindness in this cold environment. "Listen," he said, leaning in slightly. "Today's test isn't as bad as it seems. They're just checking basic skills, nothing too crazy." He glanced toward the glass window overhead. "I'll be up there, watching over you. I won't let them do anything too extreme."

I wanted to believe him. His words gave me a sliver of comfort, but it wasn't enough to quell the anxiety gnawing at my insides.

"I'll be rooting for you," Michael said with a weak smile. Then he pointed toward the viewing chamber before rushing off.

I stood alone in the massive arena. My heart pounded in my chest as dread clawed its way through me. Suddenly, a voice boomed through the speakers.

"Bring in TS1M3!"

The command sent a chill down my spine as the massive door groaned open. Instinctively, I backed away, my heart racing. A foul, pungent smell filled the room as a massive creature lumbered into the light.

At first glance, it resembled a honey badger, but its size and armoured hide were terrifyingly unnatural. Its skin was segmented, like an armadillo's, and its long, scaly tail lashed out menacingly.

I kept backing away, hoping for some kind of escape, but when my back hit the cold metal door, I realized there was no way out. The door was locked.

Panic gripped me as the creature let out a low hiss and charged. I bolted to the side, adrenaline surging through my veins, every instinct screaming at me to run. The creature swerved, its claws skidding against the metal floor, and its tail smashed into the wall with a deafening crash, denting the metal. Sparks flew as the damaged door creaked open slightly, offering a glimmer of hope.

Desperation fuelled my movements as I raced around

the perimeter of the arena, my breath coming in short, frantic bursts. The creature's growls echoed through the air, each sound a reminder of the danger just behind me. I was running out of time.

I reached the damaged door and tried to push it open, but before I could escape, the creature's tail whipped through the air. I felt a sudden impact, and the next thing I knew, I was crashing into the opposite wall. Pain exploded through my body as I slid to the floor, blood filling my throat as I coughed weakly. Each breath was agony, my chest burning with every inhale.

Through the haze of pain, I saw the creature again, its massive form looming over me. But just as it prepared to strike, something stopped it. The beast trembled violently before collapsing to the ground, motionless.

Exhausted, I sank to the floor, my vision swimming. At last, the world faded, and I closed my eyes to rest.

# CHAPTER FIVE

## TESTING

I didn't know how long I'd been out. When I finally came to, I found myself lying in a hospital bed. My midsection was bandaged tightly, the pain throbbing with every shallow breath. I couldn't sit up, couldn't even move without a jolt of soreness running through my body. Carefully, I turned my head, taking in my surroundings— sterile white walls, the sharp smell of antiseptic hanging in the air.

"Hey, you're up," a voice came from the side.

I slowly turned my head in the direction of the voice. Michael. He stepped closer, his expression a mixture of relief and worry.

"You were out for half a day," he said, his voice soft. "Which is weird because the first two... they were only out for about five hours when it happened." His eyes darted away for a moment before he caught himself. "Oh, sorry. Forget what I said. It's nothing."

He must've seen the confusion in my face, but I was too tired to ask what he meant. Too drained to even care.

"You really took a beating," he continued, moving to sit in the chair beside my bed. "That badger... it really did a number on you. How are you feeling?"

"I...I..." My voice was hoarse, barely a whisper.

"Hold on, let me get you some water." He quickly stood up, disappearing for a moment before returning with a jug and a glass. He filled it and walked over to me, carefully sliding a hand under my neck to help me sit up. "Here, use the straw." I nodded weakly, grateful for the cool water as it soothed my parched throat. I sipped slowly, each swallow a small comfort. When I'd had enough, I turned my head away, and he set the cup down on the table beside the bed.

"I'll leave it here for you in case you want more later," he said with a smile, though it didn't quite reach his eyes. He looked tired. We both were.

"How are you feeling?" he asked again. "Better," I rasped, though the word felt like a lie.

"Good," he replied, nodding. "You'll probably be fine enough to walk in a few hours anyway."

I frowned. "How?"

"That's just how it goes here," he said, almost too casually. "You'll heal fast. That's the way they've made it.

42

The tests, that's what they're for."

"Okay..." I muttered, not fully understanding but too exhausted to question it.

"You don't talk much, do you?" Michael chuckled softly, though there was no humour in it. "It's okay. I'll be here if you need anything. I'll stay until you're well enough to walk around again."

True to his word, within a few hours, I could stand. The soreness still lingered, but my body felt stronger, as if the injuries were already mending themselves at an unnatural pace. It was unsettling, but by now, nothing in this place felt normal.

...

Weeks passed. I found myself back in my room, waiting for Michael to collect me for another test. I had woken earlier than usual and decided not to fight for more sleep. I knew what was coming. I'd been through enough drills and practice sessions to prepare for what they called "better results." The knock came after hours of waiting.

"Hey, it's me," Michael's familiar voice called. "How are you feeling today?"

"Fine," I replied, though my stomach churned with

43

dread.

He unlocked the door, and I stepped out to join him in the hallway. After a quick stop in the medical wing for a routine check-up, he led me down a different corridor than usual. This time, his expression was more relaxed, and he even managed a small smile. But the pit in my stomach only deepened as we descended further into the facility—the place I had come to think of as the home of my nightmares.

This time, the creature waiting for me was no badger. Emerging from the dark, towering door was an insect-like beast, as large as a peacock, the black and yellow stripes on the abdomen reminded me of a bee or wasp. Its wings buzzed with a menacing hum. The black collar around its neck signified what I already knew—it was another one of their creations, just like the badger.

Before I had time to react, it lunged.

I dodged, but not fast enough. Its stinger shot forward and grazed my arm. The pain didn't explode immediately like the last time. Instead, it built slowly, intensifying in that single spot, burning hotter and hotter until it felt like the skin was melting away. I screamed.

I had learned to run, just like before. The training had been brutal, but it taught me how to move. And I needed to keep moving if I wanted to survive. My mind raced.

The bee was fast—much faster than the badger had been. Its eyes, a multitude of them, were trained on me, its movements calculated, its tail striking with precision. It didn't just swing wildly; every motion was deliberate.

I needed to think. I needed to figure out how to stop it.

But my arm...my arm was going numb. The venom, or whatever poison was in the sting, was spreading quickly. I could feel it crawling up my shoulder, my muscles freezing as it moved. I couldn't fight like this. Not when my own body was betraying me.

Then it struck again. This time, the stinger hit my right leg, sending a wave of paralysis through me. I stumbled, my legs buckling beneath me. The pain shot through my body like wildfire. I was on the ground now, my vision blurring from the agony. I looked up and saw the creature's stinger, ready to strike again. Not again. I tried to move, but the numbness had taken hold of me. My limbs wouldn't respond.

The world didn't slow down as the stinger came for me one more time. Everything happened in a blur. One moment, I was willing my body to move, desperate for something—anything—to stop the attack. The next moment, the bee's tail was gone. It lay twitching on the ground, severed from the body.

I blinked, my mind struggling to process what had just happened. The bee itself buzzed frantically, but it didn't last long. Its body trembled before collapsing in a heap, lifeless.

I didn't pass out this time. The fire within me still burned, though not from adrenaline. The poison was still coursing through my veins, but something had changed. I wasn't sure what.

A face appeared before me, though everything was blurred now. I felt like the world was spinning, shaking beneath me. Colours danced across my vision—black, white, green. My mind wandered.

Bruno? Why... why did you bark? You should've kept quiet. Mom said so too. But you didn't listen. You never listened...and the green took you away. Run...run away from the green.

Everything was white now. Then black. The black was spreading, framing everything. Soon, it swallowed me whole, and everything went dark.

## CHAPTER SIX

## TAKING ANOTHER LIFE, MORE TESTING

Michael moved swiftly, his heart pounding in his chest as he helped lift Taranis onto the waiting stretcher. The boy's face was a whirlwind of emotions—ecstasy one moment, confusion the next. He sobbed, muttering incoherent words, only to suddenly grow silent, his body trembling with fear before slipping back into a state of wild excitement. The rollercoaster of emotions finally ended with him going limp, like a marionette whose strings had been cut.

Michael stayed by his side, running alongside the stretcher as they hurried toward the medical wing. He glanced down at the boy, whose expression shifted between dazed horror and uncomprehending bliss. What was he seeing? He thought as he watched the boy.

Michael knew the venom of that bee caused hallucinations as well as having a paralytic effect, the victim would either be in bliss or complete horror as they were devoured painlessly.

Hours later, after the medical staff had finished

tending to Taranis, Michael sat in the same chair he'd used the last time, watching over the boy as he slept. His orders were simple: stay with the test subject. But the job came with a shadowy weight. The last two soldiers assigned to similar roles had been mangled beyond recognition when their subjects lashed out and escaped. They had both died on the spot, their bodies unrecognizable. The rumours haunted him, but he couldn't abandon the kid now. He reminded him of his family, those he was fighting for.

The door creaked open, and Michael's head snapped up. Dr. Simmons entered, flanked by four military personnel, their expressions as cold and distant as their sharp uniforms.

"Strap him down," Simmons ordered.

Michael immediately stood up, moving to block the path of the soldiers. "What are you doing?"

"Stand down, Michael," Simmons replied, his tone even but firm. "The subject is dangerous and currently unstable." Michael's heart skipped a beat. "Unstable?"

Simmons' eyes were hard, betraying no emotion. "We reviewed the footage from the M5 test. Subject killed it — using quills.

Michael blinked, confused. "Quills?" "Yes. Quills.

48

Now, step aside."

For a long moment, Michael hesitated, conflict twisting in his chest. His instinct screamed at him to protect Taranis, but Simmons's authority loomed large, unshakable.

Finally, he stepped aside, watching as the soldiers approached the bed.

The doctor moved to the side of the bed, reaching underneath to adjust something. The bed extended, making room for straps to secure Taranis. The soldiers wasted no time, fastening the belts around the boy's wrists, ankles, and chest. Once they finished, they left without a word.

Simmons lingered by the door, his voice low as he addressed Michael. "The quills came from inside him, Martin. When we retrieved them, they were coated in poison." He paused, letting that sink in. "None of us saw it happen. One moment M5's tail was about to strike, and the next, its tail was severed. M5 was dead. We cannot afford to let this happen again."

And with that, Simmons left as swiftly as he had arrived, leaving Michael standing alone, staring down at the restrained boy.

...

**Taranis**

When I woke, I was alone in one of the testing rooms. My head throbbed with an intensity that made my vision pulse with each beat of my heart. I groaned, shifting slightly, but the restraints held me in place.

I wasn't alone for long. The door opened, and Tracy entered, clipboard in hand as always. She barely looked at me as she approached the bed, making notes on her clipboard.

"Record time," she muttered, scribbling something down.

Her footsteps were loud against the metal floor, the sound echoing in my head. Everything was too loud. I tried to focus on the beat of my own heart, but the rhythm of her steps only added to the cacophony in my skull. As she stepped away, I made a mental note to check her feet the next time she left. For some reason, the idea of focusing on something so mundane made the chaos in my mind feel more manageable.

"Good timing," she remarked, her voice as flat as always. She left the room without another word, but I could still hear her outside the door, her footsteps blending with another set—someone else was joining her. They whispered, but my head was still pounding too hard to make out the words. When she came back, she was alone.

"Begin," Dr. Simmons's voice boomed over the intercom. The sound pierced through my skull like a knife, and I winced, though Tracy didn't seem to notice the way it affected me.

She pulled out a severed stinger—probably from another one of their mutated insects—and jabbed it into my arm. I winced at the sharp pain, but I didn't scream. I'd learned not to. The familiar, burning sensation spread through me, but this time, it didn't incapacitate me the way it had before. After a few moments, the pain subsided, leaving me weak but still able to move.

"It worked, Dr. Simmons," Tracy said, her voice laced with a hint of pride as she looked at me.

"That's not necessarily a good thing, Dr. Phils," Simmons's voice responded through the speaker.

"Very well. We'll continue with the physical tests," she said, her tone returning to its cold neutrality.

A short while later, Michael came to release my restraints. He helped me up, his face tense but relieved. "Let's get you back to your room," he muttered quietly.

...

This time, the creature they released wasn't a badger— it was larger, with a massive, scaly tail that swung like a whip. A mutated beaver, its powerful tail the primary weapon, its tail looked more like a whip than the generic paddle shape. The familiar black collar was wrapped around its neck, and something else was different this time. It had a collar too. I'd been warned. Fight back, or the collar detonates.

The room was filled with the sound of the creature's heartbeat, a steady, rhythmic thrum, clear as running water. Each time the beaver swung its tail, there was a brief window when it left itself defenceless. I just had to find a way to close the distance without getting killed.

My body had other plans.

I dodged its first strike, the massive tail just missing me. Somehow, as I evaded, something sharp shot out from my body—quills, like before. I was so shocked I barely registered the next strike until I was already flying across the room, the impact sending a jolt of pain through me. I'm getting used to being tossed around, I thought grimly as I struggled to stand.

The beaver was massive, but it moved with surprising speed, each swipe of its tail calculated and deadly. I grappled for that feeling again, the one that had triggered the quills. The memory of it was faint, but as I dodged another attack, it came back, more quills shooting from my body. They struck the beaver, embedding themselves in its thick hide.

It let out a long, frustrated chitter, spinning toward me with fury. But its movements were slowing, and I knew I had to press my advantage. Each round of quills seemed to weaken it, and as it staggered toward me, I realized the tide had turned. A few minutes later, it collapsed. I walked toward it cautiously, my heart still racing. The creature lay still, its breaths shallow. I could hear its heartbeat slow, and when I was close enough, it stopped completely.

The beaver was dead.

And my nights were to be haunted by its final moments—the slow beat of its heart echoing in my mind, a constant reminder of the life I'd taken.

# CHAPTER SEVEN

## IT ALL CAME CRASHING DOWN

A week had passed since my last encounter in the arena, the physical training continuing relentlessly. Training had become routine—target practice, more injections, and check-ups. The motions had become mechanical, each day bleeding into the next, my mind numbing to the repetition.

Then, everything erupted.

I awoke to the deafening wail of alarms blaring throughout the facility. My body jolted awake, heart hammering in my chest. Screams, gunshots, and guttural growls filled the air—a chorus of chaos. Panic set in immediately. I curled into a corner of my room, pulling my knees to my chest as I pressed my hands over my ears, trying to shut out the cacophony outside.

Suddenly, the door to my room burst open, slamming against the wall. Michael stood in the doorway; his face wild with urgency. "Taranis, get out, now!" he yelled, his voice barely audible over the blaring alarms.

I shook my head, too terrified to move. My body stayed rooted to the spot; hands clamped over my ears as if that would somehow make it all disappear.

Michael let out a frustrated growl, stomping into the room and yanking me roughly to my feet. His grip was firm, almost painful, as he dragged me toward the door.

"Go up the stairs at the end of this hall," he shouted, pointing ahead. "When you emerge, turn left. There's another hallway—third door opposite where you come out. It'll lead you outside. The others will be waiting. Go!"

"I-I-I can't," I stammered, my voice barely more than a whisper. My throat was raw, the words catching in my throat. Is that really my voice? I barely recognized it, weak and frail.

Michael's eyes blazed with frustration, but beneath the anger, there was something else—fear. "Listen to me, Taranis. There's not much more I can do for you, but I'm giving you a chance to escape. Get to one of the cars outside, or stay and hope they don't find you." He glanced down the hallway, his tone growing more desperate. "But you need to go, now!"

Escape? His words didn't make sense. Why would he help me escape? They had spent every day pushing me to the brink with those tests, those injections. Yet, here he was, offering me a way out.

"GO!" Michael bellowed, his voice shaking with urgency.

I hesitated for only a second longer before my body, driven by the instinct to survive, finally obeyed. I ran. Behind me, I heard a monstrous roar, followed by rapid gunfire. My heart leapt into my throat, and my legs pumped harder, propelling me down the hall.

As I emerged into the second corridor, the floor trembled beneath me. The ceiling groaned, then gave way, chunks of debris crashing down. I wasn't fast enough. My foot caught on the uneven floor, sending me sprawling just as the ceiling caved in completely. Heavy rubble pinned me to the ground, the impact jarring every bone in my body.

Pain seared through me, but I couldn't move. My limbs were trapped, the weight of the debris pressing down, crushing me. Exhaustion washed over me like a heavy tide. As much as I fought to stay conscious, my body gave in. The world around me dissolved into darkness.

When I woke again, everything was a blur. Pain radiated through every part of me, but my body refused to move. My eyes fluttered open, but my vision was hazy, disoriented. Where am I? I strained to make sense of my surroundings, but it was difficult. I was still buried beneath the rubble. They hadn't found me.

Through the haze, I heard faint scuttling nearby—small animal, perhaps, or something far more sinister. My mind raced, heart pounding against my ribcage. Please, let it be animals.

A loud thud echoed down the hall, sending a shiver through my battered body. I tensed, every muscle screaming in protest. Pain surged again, ripping through me. I tried to lift my arms, to push the rubble off, but I was too weak. Darkness crept in from the edges of my vision once more, and this time, I couldn't fight it.

## Valerius

It had been only a month since the base fell. Scavenging was a risk, but it was either that or retreat—and we couldn't afford to retreat. We were running out of everything. I knew coming here was impulsive, but it was a gamble I was willing to take.

"Ash, see anything?" I asked, keeping my voice low. She crouched beside me, her binoculars scanning the decimated base.

She shook her head. "Nothing yet."

We'd been watching the base for a week now. Occasionally, a few creatures would emerge—twisted, mutated things. But one, a massive fox-like creature, had gone back inside and hadn't come out since. Its cries were unsettling, eerie. It moved silently despite its size, its retracted claws leaving little trace. I had never seen anything like it, and its appearance had left an uneasy knot in my stomach, it had an extra set of legs and its skin was pink and fleshy rather than furry.

"Where's Cameron?" I muttered, scanning the area.

My gaze settled on him, not too far from the entrance to the base. What had once been reinforced steel doors now lay crumpled and shattered about 20 meters from the building. Whatever had destroyed them had done so with incredible force.

Ash didn't respond, too focused on her task. Cameron, who was inching closer to the base, was the only one risking getting closer. A few more moments passed before Ash finally stowed her binoculars. "All's clear. Let's go."

She stood, dusting herself off, her hand instinctively brushing against the gun strapped to her hip. She moved ahead without waiting for me.

I followed, rolling my eyes. She's always in a hurry.

The base was worse inside than I had expected—

glass shards littered the floor, bloodstains smeared across walls and metal debris sticking out from every angle. The low hum of machinery still reverberated through the building, like a dying heartbeat.

"What's that sound?" Ash whispered.

I glanced at her. "Probably that thing I saw yesterday." Her eyes narrowed. "You mean it's still here?"

I nodded, keeping my voice low. "Enough talking. Ash, check the offices. I'll search the containment areas. Cameron, look for food and medicine. No detours, and if anything looks off, leave it."

They both nodded before disappearing down different hallways. I moved cautiously through the empty cells, my steps echoing loudly in the eerie silence. Each room was the same—bare, untouched since the collapse. No one left alive here, there was however one room that had some rotten food and a bucket, I guess they had at least one test subject here.

Further down, I found a few guns, a researcher's journal, and some water bottles. Better than nothing, I thought, packing them up and turning back toward the entrance. Then, a loud thud reverberated through the building.

I froze, listening. The sound echoed through the walls. I moved quickly, the low hum from earlier gone now, replaced by scraping. It's awake. I bolted for the stairs, heart pounding as I ascended two steps at a time. Above me, I heard footsteps. Ash. She was moving just as fast. We burst out of the stairwell at the same time, rushing toward the end of the hall. "CAMERON!" Ash yelled, her voice giving away our position. He stomped twice, signalling he had found something—or someone.

"There's someone trapped here!" Cameron's voice echoed back.

"Are they alive?" Ash called out. "Yes!" he shouted.

"Hurry up! The thing I saw yesterday knows we're here!" I barked, glancing nervously down the hall.

Ash didn't hesitate. She sprinted toward Cameron's direction while I stayed behind, keeping watch. We didn't have much time. Moments later, they returned—but without whoever was trapped. Cameron's face was set in determination. "We need more strength."

I cursed under my breath but nodded. He won't leave them behind. "We'll have to be quick." I listened for the scraping sound—it was getting closer, but we had time.

Together, we raced toward the trapped figure. A pile

of concrete and debris covered him, his right arm bent awkwardly beneath the weight. But strangely, that seemed to be the only injury.

"We need to get him out," I said, crouching down to inspect the rubble. With the three of us working together, we pried the largest chunk off and quickly cleared the remaining debris.

The figure stirred as we pulled him free, his breath laboured but steady. With Ash's help, we got him onto my back, his body limp as we made our way toward the exit. The monster hadn't reached us yet, and I exhaled in relief as we reached the sunlight.

Cameron secured the unconscious figure to my back, tying a cloth around us to keep him steady. I nodded my thanks and we began the trek back to the camp. We had survived, for now.

# CHAPTER EIGHT

## MORE PEOPLE

### Taranis

The pain had dulled to a distant throb now, a strange contrast to the darkness that seemed to envelop me. Where am I? My mind fumbled through the haze, trying to latch onto something concrete. Footsteps echoed softly, voices murmured in the distance. Did they come back for me? Questions spun in my head as I fought to make sense of my surroundings using the few sounds around me.

I jolted awake, regretting the sudden movement immediately as a sharp pain flared through my body. I lay still for a moment, allowing my senses to adjust. As I scanned the room, I realized I wasn't in the base anymore. This wasn't a cell or a lab. The space around me looked more like a bedroom, judging by the personalized items scattered around—a wardrobe plastered with stickers, clothes folded neatly on a chair, and a single painting hanging crookedly on the opposite wall. The blanket I had been covered with had slipped to the floor.

That smell... food?

I could feel my throat, dry and scratchy, making it difficult to swallow. My eyes stung from exhaustion, my ears felt hot, and the dull throb of pain now seemed to concentrate in my right hand. Glancing down, I noticed it was wrapped in bandages—sticks in place of a cast. A cloth sling supported the injured limb, resting gently against my chest.

Footsteps approached. I flinched.

"Whoa, easy." The voice came before the figure appeared fully. I jerked back, pushing myself into the wall, knees drawn up defensively. The sharp movement sent waves of pain crashing through my sore muscles, but I barely registered it. My hair fell into my eyes, shielding me from the figure before me as a hand landed softly on my shoulder, trying to calm me.

"I'm not going to hurt you," the voice promised, gentle and soothing, like someone trying to coax a frightened animal. My heart pounded in my chest, loud enough that I was sure he could hear it. He knows I'm scared. He must.

"Well, um, I'm Cameron—Cam for short." He spoke awkwardly, reaching out, but stopped short as another voice interrupted.

"Leave him alone, Cam. You're just making it worse."

This new voice was feminine, but with a rough edge, coming from the same direction Cam had appeared.

"I wasn't—" Cam began to defend himself, only to be cut off by yet another voice, more authoritative this time.

"Enough, both of you. Cam, go eat. I'll talk to him." This voice was calmer, slightly farther off, but the weight of authority was unmistakable.

Cam sighed, defeated. "Okay."

I watched through the curtain of my hair as his legs disappeared from my view, his footsteps retreating. But another set of footsteps came closer. Whoever had spoken last was standing right in front of me now, though I couldn't see them clearly.

"How are you feeling? We were all worried about the state we found you in. Ash and Cam wanted to check that you were okay." The voice was steady, patient. "I'm Valerius, but you can call me Val. It's okay if you don't feel like talking yet. When you're ready, you can come over and eat. You're welcome here."

The words hung in the air for a moment before he, too, walked away, leaving me alone with my thoughts once again. I listened to his footsteps as he left, slowly I realized that apart from the footsteps, there were familiar rhythmic sounds echoing in my ears. Heartbeats, just like at the base, I could hear unusually better.

Hours passed. I sat curled up in the same position, right arm pulsing with dull pain, too weak or afraid to move. But eventually, the hunger gnawing at my insides became too much to ignore. Slowly, I unfurled my body, placing my feet on the floor and tried to stand.

The ground seemed to tilt beneath me. My legs gave out before I could steady myself, and the world lurched as I crashed to the floor.

"Shit," someone cursed nearby. More footsteps— Cam again. He knelt beside me, gently brushing my hair from my face, his hand steady and kind. I flinched at the touch, but he didn't pull away.

"Can I help you up?" His voice was soft, almost apologetic, and when I met his gaze, I was startled by the depth of his blue eyes. They were like lapis lazuli—clear and vivid, a stark contrast to his wavy brown hair that fell messily around his face. I nodded hesitantly.

With a small smile, he reached out, and though I flinched again, he didn't rush. When I was ready, he helped me to my feet, though my legs were still shaky. Leaning heavily on him, I let him guide me back to the bed, where he gently lowered me down.

"You okay now?" he asked, watching me closely. I nodded once more.

"Did you get up to eat? Shall I bring you some food?" I nodded again, and his face brightened as he hurried away.

He returned with a bowl of soup and a glass of water. "Do you need help with it? Your hand..." He trailed off awkwardly, but I shook my head. I could manage. He handed me a spoon, and I balanced the bowl carefully between my legs, focusing on the simple task of eating. Cam didn't try to help, even when he saw me struggle, and for that, I was oddly grateful.

...

Two weeks passed, and I had settled into a tentative routine in the apartment. I wandered through the small space, my right arm mostly healed now—the make shift cast was long gone but I had to pretend it still hurt at times so as to lower suspicion a little—, I wore Bruno's dog tag around my neck, constantly fidgeting with it—Cam, Ash's younger twin, noticed that I was always stroking it so he got me a chain to make it into a necklace.

I hadn't spoken a word to anyone yet, and though

Valerius, Cam, and Ash occasionally asked if I was okay, they seemed content with my silence. They didn't push for answers, and for that, I was thankful. I wasn't ready to talk —not about what had happened, not about who I was.

...

One day, I sat at the dining table, watching Cam wash dishes. Valerius had been in and out of the apartment all day, and Ash was out scavenging as usual.

Valerius entered the room, his presence a quiet, steady force. "Any word from Ash?" His sudden voice made me jump, my nerves still raw.

"She's on her way back," Cam replied without turning. How did he know? I wondered, I could hear her footsteps approaching, could he? "Good. I'm heading to 203. Call me when she gets here," Valerius said, turning to leave. But then, another set of footsteps approached. Ash.

**Valerius**

It's been two weeks since we brought him back. He's still jumpy, and I'm sure he has nightmares—because he avoids sleeping as much as he can, and when he does it's for a short amount of time---, but he's less tense than before. He watches us work, sometimes even helping with

67

small tasks, though he keeps his distance, still not speaking.

We've taken to speaking softly whenever we're in the same room with him, trying not to startle him. But even then, he still jumps whenever someone talks. He always absentmindedly strokes the dog tag around his neck— probably a pet, I think, though I've never asked. He squeezes it tightly whenever he's startled.

He stays inside the apartment mostly, never venturing outside the building. He doesn't sleep well—if at all. He's always awake when I check on him, and the dark circles under his eyes are growing worse. It worries me, but I don't want to push him too hard.

I walked into the apartment, I watched as Cameron was carefully taking note of the supplies we had, focusing on the medical equipment, while Ash was sat opposite him tinkering with something I couldn't name, and our latest member was sat next to Cam passing him objects and helping him with taking inventory. Occasionally he'd switch and slide over to Ash as she asked him to pass something for whatever she was creating or fixing, I couldn't quite tell. He looked up at me as I walked in before turning his attention back to Ash.

"Hey guys, we're leaving tomorrow so get packed by tonight okay. Cam's on Watch."

...

Later that night, as I was packing, a gunshot sliced through the quiet. My heart leapt into my throat.

Cameron. Grabbing my gun, I bolted from my room, rushing next door. I threw the door open and found him— our latest member—already awake, a knife clutched tightly in his hand, eyes wide with fear.

"Sorry," I said, trying to stay calm. "We need to leave. Are you packed?" He nodded, and I shot him a small smile, zipping his bag for him before gesturing for him to follow me. We descended two floors before we found someone—Ash, equally tense. "Cameron..." I breathed, fear twisting in my gut.

We stumbled into the reception, where Cameron's bag lay abandoned. But there was no sign of him.

# CHAPTER NINE

## HE SPEAKS

### Cameron

Scouting is great, but being on lookout is even better. Up here, on the roof, I get the clearest view of the creatures that now roam this world—most of them twisted products of human curiosity. Scientists, in their thirst for knowledge, brought us to this point, but I don't mind. I've always liked animals, even the ones that could easily kill me.

Ash would lose it if she knew I was up here alone. She's always telling me to be careful, but what she doesn't know won't hurt her. A cold shiver runs down my spine when I spot movement—a scai creeping towards our building. The survivors we met before called them that, a name meant to remind us why the world turned to chaos in the first place.

"This isn't good," I mutter.

I steady my breath, take aim, and count down. "3… 2… BANG." The net shoots out mid-air, capturing the creature —a giant centipede, its huge mandibles vibrate as it screeches unhappily, I grin to myself. Got it.

I quickly scan for a way down. Windowsill it is. Slinging the gun over my shoulder, I jump down and make my way back to the others.

By the time I reach the reception, the rest of the group is already there.

"Hey there, strangers," I greet them, waving. "What did you kill?" Val asks as he approaches.

"Nothing," I reply, confused. "Why would you think that?" "The gunshot," Val responds, clearly expecting more.

I roll my eyes and grab my bag from him. "I didn't kill anything. But if you're asking if we need to leave, then yeah, we should. I trapped it, but once it breaks free, it won't care who's a threat and who's food."

Ash walks past me without a word, and I follow her out.

### Taranis

We've been walking for hours, the moon casting just enough light to guide us. I'm scared. A cold shiver runs down my spine, and I pull my jacket tighter around me. Suddenly, I bump into Cameron. He steadies me without even turning around.

"There's a scai up ahead," he whispers.

"Everyone down," Val calls from the front. He

crouches behind a nearby car, and we all follow suit.

My heart pounds as memories of my mother flood back. Not again. Please, not again. I struggle to keep calm, but the fear is overwhelming.

Ash pulls me to my feet and tugs me forward. I glance around, noticing that Val and Cameron are ahead, jogging towards the next building. Slowly, I regain control of my legs and start running with her. We catch up to the others, and I bend over, gasping for breath.

Cameron crouches in front of me, looking up with concern. "You good?"

I nod, still trying to catch my breath. He nods back and stands up.

A sudden, unearthly shriek pierces the air, and I instinctively cover my ears. I'm shaking, but not from the cold. In fact, I realize I don't feel the cold at all, even though it must be freezing out here. What's happening to me?

"Shit, dawn's breaking," Ash points out. "Everyone inside that building!"

We crouch behind some old furniture, and when Cameron pulls me down behind a reception desk, I fell flat on my backside. But I don't care. We need to stay hidden. We sit in silence for what feels like hours. The sun has risen, but none of us move. I open my mouth to speak.

"Clear," Ash calls softly from her hiding spot.

Cameron gestures for me to stand, and I do. Ash points toward the emergency stairs on opposite sides of the building. Valerius and Cameron nod, and we split into pairs. I follow Cameron while Ash goes with Valerius.

There's blood on the steps as we ascend, but I force myself to focus on Cameron's back. Don't think about it. I try to push the thoughts away, but a knot forms in my stomach. Was that…the liquid they injected into me? I shake my head, trying to clear it. Sleep. What I need is sleep.

…

The nightmare started like the others.

I wake up in the base. The walls are cold metal, and my body feels heavy. Lydia stands at the door, her face expressionless. She gestures for me to follow. We walk slowly through long, empty halls, passing countless doors. There's no sound except for the faint tapping of footsteps. Suddenly, Lydia stops. Her head turns 180 degrees, but her body stays still. She's smiling, but it's not her smile. Bruno's face. "Go on," she says, her voice wrong, distorted.

73

"Dad?" I hear my father's voice, but it's coming from Lydia's mouth.

"Go on," she repeats, pointing toward a door that wasn't there before. There's a tapping sound coming from beyond the door.

I hesitate, looking from her to the door. Her face is Bruno's now, his eyes wide and unnerving.

"Go on," she urges.

I open the door. Mom. She's standing there, but she's getting further away. I try to move toward her.

"Mom?" She doesn't respond.

"MOM!" I start running, but I can't get any closer. She's fading away.

Someone's yelling. No, barking.

I turn. The creature with Lydia's body and Bruno's head is barking. The soldier who killed Bruno stands beside it, gun raised.

I want to move, but I can't. I'm frozen in front of the door.

The barking grows louder. The tapping, too. There's a scream. I whip back around, and my mom is melting again, just like before. I realize the tapping was coming from her.

74

I wake up drenched in sweat, gasping for breath. The room is dark and silent. My heart races as I stumble to the bathroom and splash cold water on my face. Just a dream. Just another nightmare.

**Valerius**

I'm in the kitchen, preparing breakfast while Cameron cleans the dining area. I've told him not to mess with my stuff, but he never listens. Ash is in the bathroom, and Taranis is sitting on the extra bed, watching us.

Suddenly, he speaks. "... My name is Taranis."

I freeze. Ash stops in the doorway, and Cameron spins around so fast I think he's going to fall over. His mouth hangs open in shock.

"YOU SPOKE! ASH, VAL—HE SPOKE! HE ACTUALLY —"

Taranis goes rigid, his hands gripping the sheets tightly.

"Hush, Cam," I warn. "You're scaring him."

Cameron steps back, sheepish. "Sorry. I'm just excited."

I turn to Taranis, who's still tense but no longer clutching the sheets as tightly. "Taranis, is it?"

He nods slowly. "Yes. It's Taranis."

75

"Well, it's nice to officially meet you, Taranis. Welcome to the group."

Taranis doesn't talk much after that. He still jumps at loud noises, and he zones out a lot. We've started sleeping in the same room so we can keep an eye on him. His nightmares aren't as frequent as I expected, but when they hit, they're bad. Whenever he wakes up suddenly, Cameron rushes to his side while Ash grabs a flashlight and heads to the kitchen. I help where I can. We've started giving him warm milk to calm him down, but he never goes back to sleep. He just thanks us and insists on taking the watch for the rest of the night.

Last night was particularly rough. He won't talk about it, though. He never does.

# CHAPTER TEN

## A SMALL GROUP

**Valerius**

"I'm worried about him," Ash says quietly beside me, her eyes scanning the horizon.

"Me too," I admit, the weight of it settling in my chest.

"At least he's eating, but if he doesn't get more sleep soon, he'll get sick." She stands, brushing the dirt off her pants. Her voice is strained, and I know she's thinking the same thing I am—Taranis is getting worse.

He's fine mostly but, he's got bags under his eyes and his movements have become sluggish.

She gets up and heads towards the store we're scouting. "I'm going inside. You keep watch," she instructs.

I nod as she slides into the building, her form disappearing into the shadows. It's been two days of scouting, and the nagging worry about leaving Cameron and Taranis behind hasn't left me. The silence of the afternoon stretches on until, finally, I hear Ash's footsteps returning.

"RUN, RUN!" she yells as she bolts towards me.

I'm on my feet before I can think, sprinting alongside her.

She catches up quickly, and we run without stopping, the wind biting at our faces.

"What was that?" I ask between gasps, lungs burning.

"There was something in there. It... you know what, let's keep running for now."

We don't stop for what feels like ages. I'm out of breath, my legs feel like lead, and my chest is on fire.

"Haven't... we gone... far enough?" I gasp, dropping to my knees, desperately trying to catch my breath.

Ash turns; her breath ragged as well. "You can't go on?" I shake my head, gulping down air. We sit in silence for a moment, both of us trying to calm down. Once I've recovered enough to speak, I look at her, voice still shaky.

"What did you see back there?"

"A centi hunter," she replies, her voice low.

The blood drains from my face. "A hunter? How did you get away?"

She avoids my gaze, and I decide to leave it alone. Pushing her now would only make things worse.

"I'm fine now. Let's head back. We've got enough supplies." She forces a small smile, though it doesn't reach her eyes.

I stand, dusting off my pants. "Lead the way," I say, returning her smile as best as I can.

Time passes quickly, and before we know it, night has fallen. The moon bathes the landscape in silver light, and nocturnal creatures stir around us. We tread carefully, trying to make as little noise as possible. After a while, we find a small intact building and decide to stay there for the night. Using whatever heavy furniture we can find, we block the entrances, eat a quiet meal, and settle down.

"I'll take the first watch," I offer. Ash nods, lying down to sleep, and I sit quietly in the dark, listening to the sounds of the night.

### Taranis

The nightmares are worse now—each one more vivid, more confusing than the last. I splash cold water onto my face, hoping to wake myself up from the endless loop of terror, but it doesn't work. Where's Cameron?

"TARANIS!"

My ears perk up at the sound of my name. I quickly tuck Bruno's tag back into my shirt as the door flings open, the loud thud echoing through the room. I flinch, heart racing.

"Ah, sorry! Sorry, my bad," Cameron says, looking sheepish. "Come with me," he gestures, his tone light.

I follow.

The afternoon sun is blinding as we step onto the roof. I raise my hand to shield my eyes, and Cameron grabs my arm, pulling me towards the shadowed side of the building.

"Look over there," he says, handing me a pair of binoculars and pointing into the distance.

I peer through the lenses and spot a few dots moving on the horizon. They're getting closer. My hands suddenly feel clammy, and my heart pounds in my chest. People.

I drop the binoculars, stumbling backward, panic rising like a wave. "No… no… not again," I mutter, breath hitching.

They're back… they came for me… no more needles… NO!" I fall, my backside hitting the ground hard. My whole body feels like it's burning. I can smell blood, though I don't know where it's coming from.

My vision blurs as the world tilts, and somewhere, far away, I hear my name. "TARANIS." Is that my mom?

**Cameron**

Taranis freaked out. This is my fault.

He hasn't left his room since the panic attack on the roof. I've tried calling for him, tried coaxing him out, but nothing. I'm pacing in front of his bedroom door, wondering if I should contact Val. He was doing fine... what happened?

When he fell, he scratched his palms, bleeding from where his nails had dug into the floor. I had to cover his mouth to calm his breathing, but even then, it took forever to get him to focus. I carried him back inside, and since then, he's locked himself away.

"Taranis, please come out." The new people we spotted from the roof are sitting at the table now, eating. They collapsed from exhaustion when they arrived, and I let them rest until dinner. Now, I watch them from my spot near Taranis's door, listening for any sound from inside.

"I'm Angel," the woman with wine-coloured hair says, finishing her meal. "This is Arin," she gestures to the boy beside her, "and this is Hope." She smiles as she cradles a baby, who coos softly in her arms. Cute.

A loud thud echoes from behind me. Is Taranis okay in there?

I quietly slip into the dark room. "Taranis? You okay?" I ask, flipping on the light. The room is silent. I look around and spot him, curled under the covers, facing the wall. The broken lamp on the bedside table catches my eye. Is he really okay?

"Hey, are you good? Don't worry, I won't ask about what happened. I'm just checking on you."

The door creaks open, and I turn to see Angel standing in the doorway.

"Uh… we just wanted to know if we should leave. You seem to be dealing with something."

"No, it's fine. Stay in your rooms for now," I reply, brushing past her into the living room. My eyes drift to Hope, sleeping peacefully in Arin's arms. Adorable.

Val contacted me finally. He said he and Ash would be back late tomorrow. I told him about the new people and Taranis's condition. He reassured me I'd made the right call letting them in and said Taranis would come around.

"He'll come out eventually," Val said, his voice calm.

"I hope so. I should have been more careful."

"You're doing fine. Just give him space. He's got his own battles."

"See you soon."

"Bye."

## CHAPTER ELEVEN

## AWAKE

### Taranis

I stare into the darkness, my body heavy, my throat sore. The quiet feels oppressive, but I don't want to sit up. Still, the questions in my mind push me forward. Where are the others? Cameron sounded worried... Who did we see from the roof? Have Ash and Valerius returned?

By the time the flood of thoughts dies down, I'm already at the door. My trembling hands press against it, and I struggle to control my breath. Just push it open.

Before I can, the door swings inward on its own, and I stumble forward, caught by an arm.

"Careful there," Ash says softly, steadying me. Her hand is firm but gentle. She watches me closely, concern etched on her face. "What are you doing? Is something wrong?"

"I..." My voice cracks. "Are you okay?"

"What do you mean?" she asks, guiding me back to the bed after flicking on the lights. The room feels too bright, too sharp.

"There...we saw people from the roof. They were coming in this direction and—"

"Oh, you mean Angel and the others?" She gently pushes me to sit on the bed, then pulls a chair from the corner to sit in front of me. Her expression softens.

"Yes...Angel, Hope, and Arin?" I ask, my voice barely more than a whisper. Her face morphs into one of surprise, she's probably wondering how I know their names. I can't tell her I heard them introduce themselves even though they weren't anywhere near me. This is all because of those tests. "Yes, Cameron told us what happened, she simply brushes off her curiosity. I'm glad he was able to help you calm down. Are you okay?"

I nod, but I don't meet her eyes. "Where is Cameron?"

"He's fine," she says, giving me a reassuring smile. Her eyes follow mine as I glance around the room, searching for some kind of confirmation. "Are you okay?" she asks again, her voice softer this time.

"I think so. When did you get back?" "Not too long ago." "What time is it?"

"It's late," she says, leaning back in her chair.

"Are you on watch?"

"No, it's my turn to check on you." "Oh."

84

I try to stand, but she stops me with a gentle hand. "Where are you going?" "I want to find Cameron. Just to make sure he knows I'm alright."

Ash nods, dropping her hand. "That's a good idea. He was pretty worried when you locked yourself away. But you're eating something first." She smiles, her tone firm but kind. I nod in agreement, too tired to argue.

We head to the kitchen, and Ash pulls a plate from the microwave, placing it in front of me. "Eat this," she says, her gaze fixed on me as I sit down.

I glance at her. "Are you just going to watch me eat?"

"Yes," she says with a grin.

I met Angel, Hope, and Arin not too long ago. Though I didn't say much, I don't think they're here to harm anyone. They seem... tired. Just like the rest of us.

...

The next day, while we're eating, I blurt out, "I want to look for someone."

Ash glances at me, raising an eyebrow. "Who?" "My father."

"Do you know where he is?" Cameron asks, his curiosity piqued.

Ash gives him a sharp look. "He wouldn't be looking if he knew where he was."

Valerius leans forward. "Where did you last see him?"

"When this all started. We were in my town. I went to help a neighbour, and then...my mom didn't make it. But my dad—he wasn't there. A gun was missing, so I think he took it. I hope he's still alive."

Valerius nods thoughtfully. "Do you have any idea where he might have gone?"

"No," I say, my voice barely audible.

"What was the name of your town?" he asks.

"Saint's Burrow."

"Never heard of it," Cameron blurts out.

"I've been through there," Angel speaks up, drawing our attention. She gestures to Arin. "We passed through it on our way here."

Hope coos softly in Arin's lap, and Angel's eyes soften for a moment before she continues. "We had someone with us then...Hope's mother."

"I'm sorry," we all say, our voices quiet and solemn.

"It's alright," Angel says with a sad smile. "I think...we may have met your father briefly while we were there."

The breath catches in my throat, and I choke on my

water. Ash immediately rubs my back, her touch grounding me as I catch my breath.

"Slow down," she says, her voice calm. I put the cup down, taking slow, deep breaths. "What did he look like? Can you describe him? Would you recognize him in a picture? What was he wearing? And if—"

"Whoa, one question at a time!" Cameron cuts in, chuckling lightly.

Angel hesitates, glancing at Arin as if searching for the right words. "He... well... Arin?"

The boy shrugs, his eyes flickering between me and Angel.

Ash steps in, sensing the tension rising. "Let's pause this for now," she suggests. "We can talk more about it tonight. For now, how about you rest up, Taranis, and let Cameron check you over, just to make sure you're alright?"

I don't argue, though my mind is spinning. I get up to wash my plate, but just as I reach the door, a shiver runs down my spine. Every hair on my body stands on end.

"Something's coming," I say, my voice barely above a whisper.

A chair scrapes against the floor as someone stands.

"What do you mean?" Ash asks, her tone cautious.

"Shh... listen."

The room falls silent, and the air feels thick with tension.    Thump, thump, thump...The sound is distant but steady. I   close   my   eyes,   focusing   on   it. Thump...thump... thump... It isn't getting closer, though. The sound is...fading. "It's dying," I say without thinking, the words slipping out.

**Valerius**

I strain my ears, but I don't hear anything. "Do any of you hear that?" I whisper to the group. They all shake their heads.

Taranis seems certain, though. He's convinced something is happening—something we can't perceive. But then he says it's dying.

"Taranis—"

A loud screech splits the air, freezing us all in place. It's sharp, unnatural, and it lingers for a moment before fading out into the night.

Taranis exhales softly. "It's dead now," he says, his voice unnervingly calm.

## CHAPTER TWELVE

## BAD AND GOOD MEMORIES

We're going back to camp today.

"Where are we going?" Angel asks as soon as we step out of the building.

"Our group is too big to keep wandering aimlessly," Cameron answers, adjusting his pack. "We're heading back to our original camp."

"Original camp?" Angel repeats.

"The three of us are scouts. We were sent to find something specific for the camp, and we've found it. So now we're returning," Ash explains.

"Will we be retracing our steps?" Taranis asks, his voice quiet. "Yes," Ash affirms, her gaze meeting his briefly.

### Taranis

We've been heading in the same direction for about eight days now, and I now realize—back when we first travelled together, they were all moving at my pace. This time, I'm struggling to keep up, but I push through. We pass our old base, the ruins of it still visible on the horizon. A shiver creeps up my spine as the wreckage comes into view. No one's mentioned what happened last night.

A familiar dread fills me. My muscles tense. A scent— one I wish I could forget—lingers in the air, sending a sharp pain through my body. No.

I stop in my tracks, paralyzed. The base looms closer, and with every step, the panic grips me tighter. No. My body trembles uncontrollably. I close my eyes, squeezing them shut, but it doesn't help. The world around me is collapsing, suffocating me.

My ears ring, and my palms press hard against them, desperate to block out the noise. There's a roaring in my head, like waves crashing violently against the shore. I can't breathe. My skin feels like it's burning, and I want to scream, but I bite my lip so hard I taste blood. If I scream, they'll hear me. They're watching. Waiting. If I take another step, they'll— "Taranis. Taranis, you're okay."

The voice cuts through the chaos, soft and reassuring, but I'm shaking too hard to respond.

"They're coming," I manage, my voice breaking.

"They're—"

"No one's coming, Taranis. If they do, we won't let

them touch you."

"You're safe, but I need you to breathe. In... out... in... out." The voice is steady, a lifeline in the storm.

"They'll find me," I gasp, panic still clawing at my throat.

A hand moves through my hair, another rubs slow circles on my back. The contact is grounding, tethering me to the present. It's not much, but it's something.

"In... out... in... out," the voice repeats. My breathing slowly matches the rhythm, and the ringing in my ears fades. The heat subsides, and my clothes feel damp and cold. My face is wet—tears, I realize.

"In... out... in... out. You're doing great. Keep breathing." The voice is right in front of me, but I can't make out the face. I just know it's familiar. Ash's scent is close, and Cameron is by my side. They're here. I'm not alone.

I sigh, the tension slowly leaving my body, though it triggers a fit of coughing. It takes a few minutes before I can stand on my own. Valerius comes over, taking my pack from me, while Ash pulls me to my feet, her grip firm but comforting.

"Here," she says, pulling a tissue from her pocket. I wipe my face and blow my nose, struggling through another bout of coughing.

"Feel better?" Cameron asks, his voice gentle. I manage a small nod, though my chest still feels tight.

"I'll walk with you," Ash offers, and I nod again. She takes my hand, guiding me as we continue. She stays on my right, blocking my view of the base as we pass its shattered doors. My heart races, but Ash's grip on my hand keeps me grounded. I focus on that—on her presence—until we've left the ruins far behind.

We find shelter in a small house, where we stay for two nights.

**Valerius**

We set out again after two nights of rest. A light shower starts, quickly turning into a downpour, but we press on until we reach Saint's Burrow.

Taranis wants to explore. He's convinced his father might still be out there. It's risky, though, and I can't help but feel uneasy. It's not that I don't understand his need for closure, but it's dangerous to put us all at risk for this.

We've all lost something in this chaos, not just him.

I can't help but think of Ash and Cameron. What if something happened to them because of this? How would we—Cameron's voice interrupts my thoughts. "You're scolding him in your head, aren't you?"

"I was just thinking about the risks he's putting us through. It could have serious consequences."

Cameron shrugs, a small smile on his face. "Everything has consequences, Val. Good or bad."

I grumble at his philosophy and march past him.

Eventually we decide to split up, much to my dismay.

## Taranis

Ash and I make our way through the streets of Saint's Burrow. The familiarity of the town stirs something deep inside me—memories, both good and bad. I lead her straight to my old house, where I show her everything, guiding her through the remnants of my past.

In the backyard, I erect a small tomb for Bruno next to my mother's. Ash watches quietly; her presence steady. As I place the final stone, she breaks the silence.

"I hope you won't have to build one for your father anytime soon," she says lightly.

I scowl, but she quickly apologizes. "I meant it in a good way," she explains, her voice soft.

We spend the night at Mrs. Greene's house, I spend that time telling Ash about my time here, in turn she tells me about how she and Cam came to meet Val before ending up at the camp. The next morning, I wake with a start, a chill running through me. I place a hand over Ash's mouth, motioning for her to stay quiet. Her eyes widen, but she nods, gently lifting my hand from her face.

She mimics my gesture, finger pressed to her lips, signalling her understanding. I can feel it—something out there, lurking. But after a few tense minutes, the feeling passes. The danger, whatever it was, is gone.

"Let's go," Ash whispers, urgency in her tone.

"We haven't found him yet," I argue, my voice tight.

"If your father's anything like you've described, he's already on his way to the nearest safe place," she reasons, her gaze steady.

"Do you know where that is?" I ask.

"No, but we'll figure it out. Information spreads. People will know about safe places. And if your father's out there, we'll find him."

"But—"

"Trust me." She pats my hair lightly before gesturing for me to get up.

## TPP (Third-Person Perspective)

The silence is shattered by a shriek. Ash spins, her eyes scanning the area.

"We should go," she says, but as she turns to face Taranis, she sees him sprinting toward the sound. She curses under her breath before racing after him.

They stop just before a clearing, where a group of people surrounds a dead baby centi, its body beaten and mutilated. The group of strangers laughs as they take turns attacking the corpse, their faces twisted in cruel amusement.

Taranis ducks behind a tree, watching. Ash catches up and hisses, "Why'd you run off?"

"I thought they might have seen my dad," Taranis whispers, eyes wide.

"Next time, say something before you leave me behind," she mutters.

"I'm sorry."

Before they can move, Ash sneezes—soft, but loud enough to catch the attention of one of the men.

"Hey! Over there!" a voice calls out.

"Shit," Ash swears, motioning for him to stay still, hoping the men wouldn't know which direction the sound had come from.

Suddenly, Ash is yanked backward by her hair.

"No!" Taranis reaches for her, but an arm wraps

around his neck, choking him. He struggles briefly before going limp, the grip loosening.

Ash is forced to her knees, the man behind her pulling her head back painfully by her hair—her hair is in a ponytail which makes it easy for him. Another man steps forward, his expression smug. "What are you two doing here?"

Taranis tries to answer, but Ash cuts him off. "We were looking for supplies. My friend's from here, and we came to check it out."

"From here, huh?" The man's smile grows wider. "That makes things easier. Bag 'em."

"What?!" Ash reacts quickly, pulling a knife from her waist and stabbing the man holding her in the thigh, over and over. He screams, releasing her, and she takes the opportunity to throw a second knife, hitting another man square in the eye. Taranis, freed, tackles the leader to the ground, landing a few solid punches before a rock slams into the back of his head, knocking him unconscious.

## CHAPTER THIRTEEN

## THIS AGAIN

**TPP (Third-Person Perspective)**

Taranis lay still on the bed, his arms and legs shackled by heavy chains. His eyes flickered open, sluggish from the drug's lingering effect, and scanned the dim room. He tugged at his restraints—testing their strength—but it was no use. Defeated for the moment, he let his head fall back against the cold metal bed frame.

The door creaked open. A woman dressed in a black tank top and cargo pants entered, moving quickly to the side to make way for another figure—a man in a lab coat.

Taranis' heart rate spiked, panic swelling in his chest. He thrashed violently against the restraints, the bed creaking under the force of his struggles.

"Call in some assistance to hold him down," the man in the lab coat ordered, his tone indifferent. The woman nodded and left. When she returned, three burly men followed her, each taking their positions around Taranis, gripping his limbs firmly.

Taranis screamed, his voice breaking as tears

streamed down his face.

"No! NO! Leave me alone! I hate it, I hate it, LEAVE ME ALONE!"

The man in the lab coat pulled out a syringe, but Taranis thrashed too violently for the needle to penetrate his skin. The man cursed under his breath, opting instead for a small vial of clear liquid. He managed to pour a portion of it into Taranis' mouth, though most of it spilled over his face.

Within seconds, the drug took effect. Taranis' screams were cut off, his body going limp as darkness swallowed him whole.

**Taranis**

When I opened my eyes again, my heart was still pounding in my chest. I scanned the room, my pulse racing with each breath, but I was alone. How long have I been here? Where are the others? Ash...

The door rattled, and despite knowing I couldn't escape, my body tensed in fear. Not again. The door creaked open, and I braced myself for the worst.

"Taranis?" a familiar voice whispered.

"Ash?" My voice came out hoarse, barely a rasp. Was it really her?

Ash stepped into the dim light, her face coming into view. Her hair fell forward, tickling my cheek as she leaned over me. "I'm here. Are you okay? What did they do to you?" Her words were a frantic whisper. "Don't worry, we'll get out of here. I'm not leaving without you."

I heard a low click and then a sudden prick in my palm made me jolt. She slipped something small and metallic into my hand, her eyes locking with mine.

"Shh... it's okay," she whispered.

"This will help you. I've unlocked your right hand— you can do the rest. They can't see you or me right now, no cameras, but everyone here is armed. There are two men right outside the door and one more outside that room."

As she speaks she gestures towards the door.

Once you're free, head down the hall to your right and keep moving. Don't look back. Hide. Wait three days. If I'm not out by then...leave."

"Ash, wait—" I croaked, but she smiled sadly and stepped back.

"I'll try to leave as soon as possible. Don't worry." With one last glance, she disappeared behind the open door, closing it quietly behind her, leaving me alone once again.

I clenched my fist around the metallic rod she had

given me, taking deep breaths to steady myself. I'll have to fight. I'll have to hurt them. The thought terrified me, but I had no choice.

With a trembling hand, I began working on the first lock.

## TPP (Third-Person Perspective)

Taranis maneuvered the small rod into the lock of his left hand's restraint, recalling what Cameron had taught him about picking locks. Slowly, the mechanism clicked, and his wrist was free. Encouraged, he sat up. His body ached, but the adrenaline coursing through him pushed him forward.

Once both his hands were free, he unlocked the restraints around his ankles and slid off the bed, his muscles throbbing. Taranis stood, testing his legs before making his way toward the door.

Ash's warning echoed in his mind. Two guards behind the door, one more outside.

His hand hovered over the doorknob, twisting it ever so slowly. He pushed the door open with all his might, slamming it into the first guard who had had his back against that very door. There was a sickening thud followed by a pained gasp. Opposite him stood the second guard, brandishing a machete. Without thinking, Taranis hurled the metallic rod at the man's face. The rod embedded itself into his eye—just as Ash had earlier with the other guy, she'd be proud of her student—and the guard let out a guttural scream before Taranis struck him with a nearby bat—it was lying on the floor after being dropped by the first guard—, sending him crumpling to the ground.

Panting, Taranis turned and burst through the outer door, tackling the third guard before he could react. The man let out a yelp before Taranis slammed the bat into his head, knocking him unconscious.

For a moment, Taranis stood there, breathless, adrenaline coursing through his veins. The world around him was a blur. Ash said to go right. He forced his legs to move, following her instructions down the hall.

At the end of the corridor, he paused, calming his racing heart. He pushed the door open, stepping into the cold night air. The cool breeze hit his face, and he inhaled deeply, his lungs burning. I'm out.

Without looking back, Taranis sprinted toward the nearest building. He ran up several flights of stairs, not stopping until he reached the top floor. Finding a room, he collapsed onto the bed, his chest heaving with sobs. The tears fell freely, hot and fast, as he buried his face in the pillow.

He cried until no more tears came, until his head throbbed, and his body ached. Eventually, exhaustion overtook him, and he drifted into a fitful sleep.

# CHAPTER FOURTEEN

## BACK ON TRACK

### Taranis

I woke up with a pounding headache and a throat as dry as sandpaper. For a moment, I stayed in bed, staring at the ceiling, trying to orient myself. But then the memory of Ash being left behind snapped me out of it. **I need to find her.**

I dragged myself to the bathroom, splashing water on my face, the coolness doing little to ease the discomfort clawing at me. There wasn't a mirror, and maybe that was for the best. I probably looked terrible.

Back on the roof, I watched the house again, hoping—praying—to see her come out. But no one had entered or left in what felt like forever. Each passing minute chipped away at my hope. What if they did something terrible to her after I escaped?

"Ash, I'm sorry," I muttered quietly, as if my words could somehow reach her. Every few hours, I found myself apologizing, wondering if she'd ever forgive me. I got us into this mess...**what if we never see each other again?**

Time blurred. The sky darkened, stars twinkling against the backdrop of the night. It was beautiful, but I couldn't appreciate it. My thoughts were a whirlwind of fear and regret. I should've stayed with her.

...

The fourth night had come, and I was dozing off at my post on the roof when a distant BANG jolted me awake. It came from the direction of the house. I shot to my feet, heart racing as I scanned the horizon.

In the distance, I saw a flurry of movement—something was happening. A cold shiver ran down my spine. No... no, not again. Frantically, I searched for the source of the danger. My body seemed to move on instinct, my gaze snapping toward a group of creatures.

But there was something worse. Insectoid figures that looked more like praying mantis accompanied the centipede-like creatures. Hunters.

I whipped around toward the house and saw Ash bolting out, running in the opposite direction of the scai. Relief and panic surged through me simultaneously. She's alive, but I must catch up to her.

I darted down the stairs and out of the building just as

Ash neared. She spotted me, a small smile flickering across her face despite the chaos. It was as if she was glad I had waited for her.

"Taranis, you waited," she panted. "We need to leave—now. They're not going to let us go."

"There are scai coming this way. I think they have hunters with them," I blurted out, the words spilling out before I could stop them.

Her eyes widened, but she barely missed a beat. "Fine, we need to go, now." She grabbed my hand, pulling me into a run. I noticed she had both of our bags slung over her shoulders. I quickly offered to carry mine, and she handed it to me without hesitation.

We ran. We ran as fast as we could, not stopping until we had gone pretty far, we then stopped when we reached a rundown gas station.

"Get some rest," Ash instructed, collapsing onto the floor. I remained standing, still reeling from the events.

"Are you hungry?" I asked, my voice barely above a whisper.

She nodded, and I fumbled through my bag, pulling out a can and a spoon. I tossed the spoon to her and rummaged for the can opener.

"No, the can opener." "Cameron."

She raised an eyebrow, her lips quirking into the barest hint of a smile. "I didn't know he had another one."

Silence fell between us again—we had already gone around and picked out what else we could find in the small store—. The tension was heavy, and I couldn't shake the shivers that crawled up my spine.

"We should leave," I said suddenly, hopping off the counter.

Ash didn't argue—I think everyone was now fine with just going along with my instincts--. She got to her feet, dusting off her pants. "You filled your bag?" she asked.

I nodded, and without another word, she took my hand. I felt a flicker of warmth at the gesture—her hand gripping mine tightly, like she wasn't willing to let me drift away.

"I don't want you to get lost," She explained quietly. "If one of us can't go on, we'll know right away."

I didn't say anything, but her grip tightened as we headed out of the building and back into the evening sky. The sun was starting to set when the nausea hit. My body began trembling uncontrollably, and I yanked on Ash's hand.

"I... I feel sick," I muttered, my stomach churning violently.

"Are you okay?" Ash's voice was laced with concern, but before I could respond, I turned and vomited.

I threw up again and again, and even long after my stomach had emptied itself. I doubled over, gasping for air as my legs buckled beneath me.

Ash knelt beside me, pulling my hair out of my face, her hand rubbing soothing circles on my back. "Are you done?" she asked softly after what felt like an eternity.

"I think so," I rasped, my head spinning. She wiped my mouth with a cloth and helped me stand.

"We need to find shelter," she said, handing me a bottle of water. I rinsed my mouth and drank greedily before washing my face. But even through the haze of exhaustion and sickness, something told me not to move.

"No," I croaked.

She stiffened. "Why?"

"I... I just think we'll be fine here."

She studied me for a moment, then nodded, not pressing further. She laid out the sleeping bags, and we settled in for the night.

Four days had passed since we escaped those thugs.

The shivers hadn't stopped, and I continued to vomit every few hours. I knew Ash was worried, though she never said it outright. We had been moving faster than normal, and I could see the exhaustion etched into her face. She wasn't just worried—I think she feared I was dying.

I think I am dying.

We had travelled so far without seeing a single soul. Ash didn't look good—she had been shot in the stomach, though she refused to let me talk about it. But the truth was obvious—she was getting weaker. If she collapsed before we reached camp. I didn't know what I would do.

I'm scared.

# CHAPTER FIFTEEN

## SOMETHING'S WRONG WITH ME

### Taranis

The camp was finally in sight, just a dark shape against the horizon. Ash had pointed it out a few hours ago, but her voice was faint, barely above a whisper before she collapsed.

I tried to stay focused, but everything felt off. My vision blurred and my legs felt like they were made of lead. Every few steps, I'd stop to check Ash, making sure she was still securely strapped to my back. I just have to keep moving. One foot in front of the other.

Almost there. I could see the intermodal containers stacked high, their shadows looming over me, offering the promise of safety.

But as I neared the camp, I noticed a figure—a hunter. Its insect body was hunched, with a dragonfly-like head and raptorial forelegs that resembled a praying mantis. Its reddish-brown skin glistened in the fading light, and its unblinking eyes followed my every move. It didn't attack, just watched.

**Keep moving. Don't engage.**

I turned, keeping my eyes on it as I backed away, waiting until I felt it was safe enough to run. When I finally reached the camp, I bolted towards the makeshift gates, the containers towering above me.

A man and a woman stood guard. The man stepped forward. "And you are?" he asked. His voice was soft, a stark contrast to his rugged appearance—shaved head, broad shoulders, and a face that screamed danger.

"Ash… she's hurt. It's bad."

"Ash?" His eyes widened as he turned to the woman, "Sam, open the gates! Ash is back!"

He reached for Ash to help, but I flinched back, instinctively jumping away. He paused, bewildered.

"Sorry," I mumbled. "You startled me."

The man simply nodded, taking my bag instead. Once inside, Ash was rushed to the medical area, and a doctor started examining her. I staggered toward the nearest restroom and emptied my stomach for the third time that day.

When I returned, Cameron and Valerius were there, their faces etched with relief. I managed a faint smile, feeling the tension drain from my body. But then, the world tilted and went black. The last thing I saw was the look of fear in their eyes as I collapsed.

### Taranis

When I came to, I was lying in a bed, my head was still spinning as I sat up and opened my eyes to chaos—people running past the open door, some were screaming as they fled in one direction, but some others were heading opposite from them with their faces set for war.

A hunter appeared at the doorway; its insect form silhouetted against the dim light. Danger. My body moved on its own, adrenaline flooding my veins. I lunged out of bed reaching for the knife that was laying on the bedside table, the creature seemed to hesitate, this puzzled me.

But then I realized it was a ploy as it sped forward towards me, I raised the knife in defence as its raptorial legs slashed at me. The knife skidded across the floor as it was knocked out of my hand in a flash, as I only just managed to dodge its follow up attack with the second 'hand'.

The distance between us was eaten up in a flash as I let my instincts take over and I only realized how close we were as my fist connected with its armoured body, knocking it back.

It screeched in retaliation before attacking once more,

but I dodged, instinct guiding me. I aimed for its abdomen and punched it again but this time my hand had plunged right through its shell, tearing out its insides. The creature let out a dying screech and went limp, I dragged my hand out of its body and wiped my hand off on the bed.

I bolted from the room, heart racing as I followed the noise of the battle.

When I reached the camp's main area, I saw the source of the panic—three giant centipedes, slashing through the camp with their hooked legs. Two more hunters accompanied them. My legs didn't slow. I charged the nearest hunter, dodging its attack before punching through its abdomen yet again—my body was moving on its own, it felt like I was a passenger as I watched what was happening through my own eyes—. It dropped with a hole gaping through its body.

The last hunter lunged at me, swiping with its forelegs. I dodged, feeling the sting of a shallow cut across my abdomen. This time I retaliated, driving my hand into its head, crushing its eye and twisting until its body dropped to the ground.

Only the centipedes remained. The survivors' gunfire barely held them back. I was about to join the fight when movement caught my eye—a survivor dragging a small scai, a baby centipede. I realized too late: this was their child. They didn't start this attack—we did.

Fuelled by rage, I snatched a discarded dagger from the ground and approached the woman dragging the baby scai. Her eyes widened in fear—she'd seen what I had done to the hunter—. "Stay back!" she warned, voice trembling.

I crouched down, cutting the rope binding the creature. It bolted toward its parents, but it hesitated. As it scurried back, avoiding fire, it returned to my feet, seeking shelter.

I thought of Bruno and my mother, the helplessness I felt when my world was torn apart. The rage surged again.

Without thinking, I stomped on the scai. Again and again, until it stopped moving. I stared at the crushed body, breath heavy. They're the reason I lost everything.

Shaking with fury, I turned to the centipedes. One was already dead, the others still battling against the survivors. My mind blanked, driven by a single, primal instinct: kill.

I charged at the centipede, sliding beneath its exposed under belly and driving my dagger through it as I slid. Its wails filled the air, a horrid symphony of pain that would have crippled me if I didn't bite down on my tongue to stay grounded.

With a final thrust I yanked the blade out before sliding out from underneath it and watched as it crumpled to the ground.

Only one left.

But as I moved toward it, I saw that the others had finished it off, bullet holes riddled its body. My heart pounded as I looked around, adrenaline still coursing through me.

Then, I saw Cameron and Valerius, standing not too far off, their expressions twisted with fear and confusion. I knew, in that moment, I had lost yet another place to call home.

## CHAPTER SIXTEEN

## HOW WEIRD IS MY BODY?

### Taranis

I've been thrown into a large cage—I don't know where it came from, and I don't think I want to know. I've been here since the last centipede was killed. Once everything settled down and everyone was accounted for, I was dragged off and left here, told to await "judgment."

I want to get out of here. There's a voice in the back of my head, taunting me, telling me I could break out easily if I tried. I shut it out, it would do me no good in this situation. I sit on the cold, hard floor of the cage and replay everything that happened. It's like watching through someone else's eyes yet again—my body moving on its own, rampaging through the camp, thriving on chaos and destruction. The memory of crushing that tiny scai under my foot replays, the sensation of its body turning to mush under my weight.

My stomach churns, but I don't vomit. I just feel...wrong.

**Seven Days Later**

A gunshot jolts me awake. I'd fallen asleep without realizing it. Blinking away the grogginess, I see a small woman with a gun pointed at me, her face twisted in disgust and rage. She missed. I hold her gaze, trying to steady my breathing as three more people approach the cage.

My heart pounds when I see Valerius with them, flanked by another man and a woman. The woman looks calm compared to the others. She's tall and lean, her toned body showing she could hold her own against the men beside her. There's no menace in her demeanour, just an air of authority that says she's in charge.

"So, you're the military abomination rescued by my scouts," she sneers, her voice calm but laced with disgust. "We can't have you here. You'll leave tonight and never come back."

She stops, studying me with a gaze that feels like it's piercing through my skin, seeing everything I am and everything I've become. "Those who wished to follow you, Ash and Cameron have been detained, along with the people Val came with. They are under examination. I don't care how Ash and her team found you, there's no pity for the likes of you here. They won't be allowed near you again.

That is all."

She turns on her heel and walks away without another word.

I shift my eyes to Valerius, desperate for some kind of reassurance. "There was nothing I could do," he says, barely meeting my gaze. "Cameron... he..." Valerius sighs deeply. "Going with you would've been too dangerous." Cameron insisted, and so did Ash. "I'm sorry, there's not much I can do for you here." He slips off his bag and pushes it through the bars.

"It's not much, but it's all I could manage."

"WAIT!" I call out as he starts to walk away. He pauses but doesn't turn around. "How's Ash and Cameron, will they be okay?"

Valerius nods without looking back, then continues on. The other guy who came with them sits down beside the cage. "I'm here until you leave," he says. "I'll be escorting you out."

I nod, resigned, and turn my attention back to the woman with the gun. She's still there, staring off into the distance, gun lowered but tension still radiating off her.

I turn my attention to the bag and examine its contents, mostly food. I simply close it after, I'll properly look once I leave.

I sit back and wait for the sun to set.

....

That night, I realise I've never really stopped to look at the night sky since everything started, and right now, it's stunning. The stars shine bright, free from the overwhelming glow of city lights, and the moon hangs unobscured by clouds. I lie on the roof of a former gas station, wrapped in a sleeping bag Cameron had practically shoved at me before I was thrown out. I thought he'd yell or cry, but he did neither. Instead, he channelled his anger into shoving people aside, barely keeping it together. The sleeping bag is almost new, soft and clean. Thanks, Cameron. I'll have to thank him if I ever see him again.

Ash had also thrown me a duffel bag over the camp's makeshift gate as they pushed me out. She called my name to get my attention, her voice strained but determined. It's not a large bag, but the supplies are enough to keep me going for a while.

I hated having to leave. The group—Cam, Ash and Val—was the closest thing to safety I'd known in a long time, but the majority had spoken, and there was nothing I could do.

As I lay under the stars, my thoughts kept drifting back to the attack.

I'd let my instincts take over, and my body had responded in ways I couldn't fully comprehend. I look at my hands, still stinging from when I'd punched through the hunter's shell. How did I even do that? I wonder. Could I do that again?

The questions swirl in my mind, tangled with fear and confusion, until sleep finally claims me.

### The Next Morning

I wake up with a single thought: I must find Michael. Or anyone from the military base. They'll know what's wrong with me.

I need answers. I need to know what they did to me, and if there's any way to undo it or at least control it.

# CHAPTER SEVENTEEN

## A NEW OBJECTIVE

### Taranis

I have no idea how I'm going to find military personnel, much less Michael or even a whole base. As I rummage through the bags Ash and Valerius gave me, I realize just how much they'd packed—food, two tactical daggers, and even clothes.   The daggers are impressive: one serrated and the other with a clean blade, both about nine inches long. They feel well-balanced in my hands, almost like short swords. I spot a crumpled piece of paper at the bottom of the bag, written messily but legible enough.

"Compass in Val's bag, head southeast, house in the woods, look for 'Aldo'. Cameron sent you."

I chuckle to myself. "Cameron sent you." It sounds more like something Ash would write. I fold the note, grab Val's bag, and find the compass, testing it to make sure it works. Packing everything back into Ash's bag, I set off, following the compass and chanting "Aldo" in my head as if it will magically lead me to what I need.

I walk for a full day, seeking shelter in a mostly

collapsed supermarket that looks like a cave made of concrete, shelves, and counters. I find a secluded spot at the back and slurp down a can of beans for dinner.

### Days Later

It's been days since I left the supermarket, and I still haven't found another intact building. I walk cautiously, avoiding places that make my skin prickle. I don't want any encounters with scai until I understand what's happening to my body. My instincts are growing stronger, and they're telling me to fight and kill, I keep unconsciously wandering towards the scai. Sometimes I stop myself just in time, my legs drawn toward danger as though they have a mind of their own.

Today is no different. I find myself hiding behind a car from a snake-spider—a monstrous creature with scales tough enough to withstand a tank shell. It's the size of a car, its black, shiny scales glistening in the sunlight. I remember Cameron explaining that these things hunt anything that creates significant vibrations. I've been hiding here for an hour, my heart oddly steady, a small comfort amid the terror.

Finally, the creature slithers away, and I slip out of my hiding spot, as I walk off, my mind echoes Ash's casual warning from the time she walked in on Cameron teaching me about all the scai he had seen.: "Some of those snake-spiders have legs; they just don't use them much." She never went into detail about that warning, and I never got the chance to ask.

The cityscape gradually shifts into a forest, tall trees blocking out most of the sunlight. After walking for a while into the woods, I spot a makeshift gate attached to a tall wall enclosing a large area. The wall is made of an eerie ring of cars, trucks, and vans stacked up, like some sort of barricade. I try to circle the structure, but the perimeter is massive.

After two weeks, I think to myself, considering how long it took me to find this place, I hope this is the place Ash was talking about.

I shiver as the hair on my arms stands up—multiple scai are nearby. I freeze when I hear a hiss.

"Not another snake…"

## Cameron

Taranis has been gone for days. And ever since she recovered, Ash has been constantly confronting Adira, the camp leader, arguing for hours in her office. This has been going on daily, Ash storming in to yell, and Adira trying to brush her off by sending her on more scouting missions. The way I see it, Adira hopes the missions will keep Ash busy. I watch Ash now, striding purposefully toward Adira's office, pushing past anyone in her way. Her expression is set in her usual mask of anger. A few days ago, Adira pulled me aside during a walk around the camp. She confessed she didn't know how else to calm Ash and asked me to talk to her.

I refused politely, biting back my own frustrations. I'm angry at Adira, sure, but I'm angrier at Valerius. He sat in on the meeting where they decided to throw Taranis out. He didn't argue, didn't defend him. I don't care that Taranis punched through the shell of a hunter or that he killed three of them. He needed support, and Valerius just watched him go.

"Cameron?" Naja, one of the nurses, calls my name, snapping me from my thoughts—I work with the health department when I'm not out scouting with my group.

"What?"

"You were zoning out. If you're not busy, go see Valerius. He'll find something for you to do."

"I'm fine. I have things to do; just not right now." "And what's that?" "Getting you to stop talking." I walk off, ignoring her annoyed huff.

I'm waiting in Ash's room while she's busy arguing with Adira, something that's been going on longer than usual today.

Ash and Arin had a run-in with a spider-snake on a scouting trip. Arin's young but surprisingly agile, fast, and a quick learner—a good partner now that Ash's previous one had voted to kick Taranis out.

There's a knock on the door.

"Who is it?"

"It's me," comes a voice I'd rather not hear. Valerius.

"I don't care. Go away."

"I need to talk to you." "I don't want to."

"You've been like this long enough."

"Like what?"

"This...attitude. The 'I don't care because you chased away my friend' attitude. I didn't chase him away. I—"

"You are part of why he's gone, Valerius. Whether you admit it or not."

"I'm sorry you feel that way, but you can't keep avoiding me. Please, just talk to me."

"I don't want to. Not today."

He sighs. "Tell Ash I'm sorry. I want to talk to you both again. We should put this behind us."

"Fine. I'll tell her you came by."

"Cameron, please."

"Just leave."

His footsteps retreat, and I finally let out a breath I didn't realize I was holding. Maybe we should talk to him. He's been apologizing a lot lately, especially since Ash gave him a black eye after finding out what happened. Not that I care, he deserved it, we spent almost two months with Taranis, he should have at least felt some guilt.

Later, Ash comes back to the room, slamming the door and heading straight to the bathroom. I hear the shower turn on.

"Ash sis, you okay?"

"Yeah," she replies with a sigh. I lie back down, trying not to fall asleep before she finishes. When she emerges, she's dressed in sweats and a tank top, her hair still damp she has a towel to it and continues drying it as she makes her way to me.

"You alright?" I ask.

"Yeah. Just thinking…should we go find him?

125

Taranis?"   "You mean leave the camp? That's practically suicide.

Besides we sent him to a good friend."

"I'd be careful."

"Ash, it's late, and you're not thinking straight. We know where he is headed, that's enough for now. Go to bed."

"You're right. But we're talking about this tomorrow."

"Fine. Good night."

"Night."

I leave her room, head back to my own, and fall into bed, the weight of everything keeping me restless despite my exhaustion.

## CHAPTER EIGHTEEN

## PROGRESS

### Cameron

Ash seems determined to leave; she's not willing to take no for an answer. I'm sure she's planning something. She's been carefully observing the camp's routines, counting hours between daily activities. I know it's only a matter of time before she attempts to escape, and I can't let that happen.

I want to go after him too, I'm worried too, but we should at least have faith and wait until everything dies down, people are still frazzled by what happened, and we have responsibilities. And why the heck am I being the sensible twin?

"Ash, Ash," I call out as I enter her room. It's been two days since I asked her to reconsider her plans to leave. She's not here, which worries me. Usually, she's either in her room, the cafeteria, or on missions. Maybe she's training.

I leave her room and head to find Matt—Ash's gym buddy.

I knock on Matt's door, and after a moment, he peeks out, yawning.

"What?"

"Have you seen Ash today?"

He thinks for a moment. "I think I saw her heading toward the gym."

"Without you?"

"Yeah."

"Thanks." I flash him a smile and turn to leave, wondering why she'd go to the gym in the middle of the day and without her buddy. I cross the small courtyard, head down the hall, and descend the stairs to the first floor. I spot Ash easily in her usual grey sweats, lifting dumbbells at the back of the gym.

I walk up to her. "Ash, I was looking for you. What are you doing in the gym?"

"Lifting dumbbells, do you need glasses now?"

I ignore her snarky comment. "It's best we don't run. We could talk to Adira, ask for permission to search for Taranis, and set a time limit. Once we find him and know he's okay, we'll come back."

"You were grumpier last time. What changed your mind?"

"I…just because?" It sounds more like a question than an answer.

"Because what?"

"I don't want you hurt or worse. Stay here, close to me, where I can keep you safe."

"You sappy little…" She trails off, her shoulders sagging. "I'm trying not to think of leaving. You've seen what's out there. Just because he killed a few hunters and a centi doesn't make him invincible.

He's only nineteen, and there are monsters with high intellect out there. He might not even be the only one like this." She whispers the last part.

"Don't forget where we found him and how we found him. There could be more bases like that. The military's capturing scai, but many still escape." She continues.

And I add, "They're capturing scai, but they're not going to catch them all anytime soon. The number of people like Taranis can't be high considering the risks."

She sighs, and I gently take the dumbbells from her. "This isn't helping. Meet me in front of Adira's office at nine tomorrow. We'll talk to her."

I smile, "You know I am worried about him too?" She nods, smiling back.

129

I nod and follow her back to her room, before heading off to find Valerius, let's put this behind us.

**Valerius**

I didn't expect Cameron to visit me at my room. After everything, I was sure he'd never speak to me again. He stands before me, glaring, the sun setting behind him. I think about watering the farm, but I decide to focus on him instead.

"We need to talk," he says sharply, stepping into the room.

I step aside, letting him in. He stands in the centre, arms crossed.

"Sure. About what?"

"Ash and I want to look for Taranis."

"That's reckless. Taranis wouldn't want you risking yourselves. He would—"

"You don't know what Taranis would feel. You chased him away. He trusted you, and you did nothing. Help us talk to Adira so we can make things right."

"It's dangerous and reckless…" I trail off but the look on his face tells me I have no choice here. "fine, I'll help however I can."

"Convince Adira to give us time to check on him."

130

You do realize if he's fine, he won't come back. You'll have to leave him on his own."

"I want to know he's okay. We've seen what's out there."

"And there are scai that don't attack on sight. He'll be fine. Stop worrying."

"Don't drag this out. We're going to meet him. That's final." He storms out, slamming the door behind him. I sigh, sinking onto my bed. At least he's talking to me.

I get up after a few seconds, better go water those plants.

...

"The surprises just keep coming," I mutter as I watch Ash striding over to me while I water the farm.

"Cam talked to you?"

"Yeah, not too long ago."

"I don't care when. We're meeting Adira tomorrow morning at nine."

"Very well."

She turns to leave, then pauses. "Cam told me you apologized. You don't need to. See you tomorrow."

Tomorrow arrives quickly. I drag myself to Adira's office, where Ash is already waiting, and Cam approaches a moment later. I smile as I get closer, but Cameron ignores me, and Ash gives me a curt nod.

"Let's get this over with," Cam says, knocking loudly on the door.

"Come in," Adira's voice calls. Cam pushes the door open and walks in, followed by Ash and me.

"To what do I owe the pleasure?" Adira's smile is cold, her eyes narrowing when they land on Ash.

"We have a request," Ash begins. "I want to see if Taranis is okay."

"That creature you dragged in? No."

"He's not a creature. He's our friend, and you didn't even give him a chance," Cameron retorts his voice rising.

"It didn't need a chance. That thing would have killed us eventually." She replies calmly, reclining slightly in her chair. "He" Cam seethes.

"What?"

"He's not an object. He's a person, whether you acknowledge it or not." Cam clarifies.

"Huh, so what? Are you trying to say I can't address it as what it is?"

Cam slams his hands on the table, his body tense as he glares at Adira who jumps at the sudden display of anger.

Cam almost never loses composure; he'll show you he's mad but he's never acted on his anger.

"HE." He says assertively, "With all due respect, I understand you have a higher standing, but if you want this conversation to go smoothly, then please address Taranis appropriately, he is a person whether you acknowledge that or not." With that he stands back, straightening himself once more.

The display got him results though; Adira sits up as she continues.

"It would have been bad if…if that boy stayed."

"You don't know that." Ash says calmly.

"I do." Adira sighs "You don't understand, none of you do." She utters this with a look of knowing, that bothers me.

"What do you mean by that?" I ask taking a step forward.

"He's not the only one of his kind. I've seen what someone like him is capable of, I don't want to see that again, not while I'm still sane." Someone like him? I didn't know much about Adira before she became our lead but clearly, I know too little.

"And what exactly was that?" I press on.

She looks up, facing me, her eyes search my own before looking away. "You can do whatever you want, find that boy or even leave for good. I hope you know what you're doing, and you'll be careful." With that she turns in her chair ending the conversation.

# CHAPTER NINETEEN

## GROWTH

### Taranis

A low growl fills the air, and a massive black cat lands in front of me, causing me to fall back onto the ground. The creature is enormous, standing almost twice my height even on all fours. It has long, twin tails that end in deadly hooks, swishing back and forth. The feline stalks toward me, its green eyes pinning me in place. I try to will myself to stand, to fight this creature as I did the centi, but nothing happens. This cat is different; it exudes a quiet, deadly power.

A sudden snap of a branch behind me makes the cat pounce, leaping over me and attacking whatever was lurking behind. The sounds of struggle and the quick swoosh of its tails fill the air, followed by a howl and a heavy thud.

When I turn around, a large canine creature lies lifeless on the ground, it's a dog in every right, but it looks like it's been skinned and on its nose are feelers like a mole.

The puma turns its gaze back to me, walks over, and effortlessly picks me up by the collar, I feel it means no harm, so I don't even struggle. It carries me toward the high wall, leaping over it with grace and landing without a sound.

The cat sets me down in front of a large house at the centre of the growth behind the wall and lets out a loud hiss before stretching and lying down, crossing its front paws elegantly. The door creaks open moments later, revealing a middle-aged woman with an air of authority.

"You are?" she asks, her voice light but with a condescending undertone.

"Taranis. I'm looking for Aldo." My voice is barely more than a whisper, and I feel unsure of myself.

"Hmm, many come here for Aldo. What is your purpose?" she asks, sounding almost bored.

"I need to find a military base. I'm looking for someone." "Why would you do something so foolish?" She studies me, her gaze sharp. "Ah, you're one of their guinea pigs."

"Yes," I admit. "I was taken and used."

"You speak as though—come in," she stops herself before stepping aside to let me in.

"You're Aldo?" I ask as I step into the house.

"Good eye." She shuts the door behind me.

"Do you know the creature outside?" I question. "Oh,

you mean Luna?" She comes and stands in front of me.

"She's like a house cat. She goes off and comes back as she pleases. Why?" She explains.

"A house cat?"

"Follow me." She leads me through her cozy but cluttered house with books scattered in a table in front of a fireplace, and a rocking chair to the side in the living room. We pass through the kitchen, where something is cooking, and descend to a basement remodelled as an office.

The walls are painted white, and there are drawings covering it, I slowly look at the art before taking in the rest of my surroundings, the large table at one end of the room, the couch adjacent to it with a smaller table in front of it and a chair too. The stone floor is clean and the window behind the huge table is closed.

"Who did you say you want to find?" she asks, her tone flippant. She's still walking ahead towards the couch.

"I haven't told you yet," I reply cautiously.

"Yes, but who?" she presses, spinning to face me. "A man named Michael."

"I don't know him, but there's a military base to the east. It'll take about a week to get there. It's been active for a while; they might have information on him," she says, settling onto the couch and gesturing for me to sit in a chair opposite her.

"Have you been there?"

"In a way," she shrugs.

"What do you mean?"

"I've met someone who needed to go there."

"You know someone at the base?"

"Maybe. The base was attacked recently, so he could be dead," she states without a trace of emotion.

"You don't care?"

"He was dangerous, bent on destruction, and would have killed me if I was of no use. So no, I don't care," she says, her calm demeanour unchanged. "He was like you."

"Like me?" I ask, shocked. The idea of others like me hadn't crossed my mind.

"Yes, another escapee from the military's experiments."

I sit there, stunned, recalling the loneliness of my time in the base. No other civilians, no other captives—just me. A small boy enters with a tray holding two mugs and a steaming kettle.

"Tea? Coffee?" she offers. "I'm fine, thanks." She shrugs and makes herself a cup of tea. "You should stay here." "What?"

"You couldn't even handle Luna. She had to carry you in like a kitten."

'Luna… the house cat.'

"Yes, her. Kane, the other like you, earned Luna's respect by defeating two snakes. Amari, who's kind yet fierce, was also acknowledged by Luna.

But you? Luna sees you as a child rather than an equal." "What happens if I stay?" I ask, wary of her intentions.

"I'll help you understand what was done to you, what your new body can do, and how to control your abilities."

I stare at her, questioning if she was once like me or if she helped the other people like me, plus I'm wary, she seemed like she wanted me to be quick and leave with her earlier attitude, so what was this sudden proposition. "You've done this before, for the other I mean?"

"I helped Amari. Kane, however, only seeks revenge. He already understood his body well."

I think about it, it wouldn't hurt, and besides that's the main reason I was looking for a base in the first place, if I can understand this body maybe I'll be able to find my father easier once I'm ready.

"I'll stay, but in exchange, help me find Kane," I decide. Learning about my abilities feels like the right step.

"Not Michael?" she asks with a sly smile.

"Yes, I want to find Kane." Someone who understands his abilities seems like a better choice to an ally of those who did this to me.

"Very well. We'll start tonight. Tavon, show our guest to his room," she calls to the boy.

...

I settle into my room as the sun sets, unpacking my few belongings. I've made my choice. "I'm sorry, Father. I'll come for you soon," I whisper to myself, determined to make sense of this new chapter in my life.

Born in London in 2005 before moving to her home country of Nigeria where she has lived most of her life. SAO loves nature in general and reading.

www.ingramcontent.com/pod-product-compliance
Lightning Source LLC
Chambersburg PA
CBHW060230180626
46813CB00007B/3029